WAGON WHEEL GAP

Center Point
Large Print

Also by Allan Vaughan Elston and available from Center Point Large Print:

Forbidden Valley
Grand Mesa
Wyoming Manhunt
Showdown
Gun Law at Laramie

This Large Print Book carries the
Seal of Approval of N.A.V.H.

WAGON WHEEL GAP

ALLAN VAUGHAN ELSTON

CENTER POINT LARGE PRINT
THORNDIKE, MAINE

This Center Point Large Print edition
is published in the year 2023 by arrangement with
Golden West Inc.

First US edition: J. B. Lippincott Company

The text of this Large Print edition is unabridged.
In other aspects, this book may vary
from the original edition.
Printed in the United States of America
on permanent paper sourced using
environmentally responsible foresting methods.
Set in 16-point Times New Roman type.

ISBN 978-1-63808-869-1 (hardcover)
ISBN 978-1-63808-873-8 (paperback)

The Library of Congress has cataloged this record
under Library of Congress Control Number: 2023938419

TO

Billy Adams of Alamosa
pioneer cattleman and
twice Governor of Colorado

WAGON WHEEL GAP

1

The wide tires of her wagon crunched in the snow-packed ruts and Helga Tarber, one strong gloved hand on the brake lever while the other held the reins, looked back to see how her load was riding. She'd looped a log chain over the thirty corral poles she was hauling down-mountain to the ranch. Each pole was a smooth spruce cylinder some six inches in diameter by fifteen feet long. Her father had cut and barked the poles last fall, leaving them stacked obliquely in the forest to dry over winter. Now, too busy with spring plowing to go after them himself, he'd sent Helga and this made her third load.

The wagon bed had been removed, leaving only the running gear with its U-shaped bracket over each axle. Into the cradle of these brackets Helga had loaded the poles, one end at a time. She was tall and strong and twenty. Since her fourteenth year she'd done a man's work—and a woman's work long before that.

This timberbound trail dipped down a ravine past the base of Horseshoe Mountain. Its narrow white aisle between piny walls was grilled by the parallel ruts Helga herself had made on earlier hauls. At the ranch, in the open valley below, there was no snow at all. Here the downgrade made easy pulling for the mules.

It was Thursday the twenty-ninth of April in the year 1880, with just enough frost to paint pink in Helga's cheeks. Of these only a little could be seen because of a woolen scarf looped under her chin and over her honey-yellow hair. Her snow boots were felt, her pants corduroy and her shirt a heavy flannel. The fleece-lined jacket she'd worn earlier in the day now lay on the load behind her. Helga herself, driving, was perched at the front of the load, the wagon seat having been removed with the bed.

"Steady, Benny-boy!" she cautioned as some forest movement or odor made the off-mule shy. Then, as the wagon turned a kink in the trail, Helga saw an obstacle ahead. Her down-rolling wagon was nearly on it before she could brake to a stop. A half-devoured doe lay in the trail with six gaunt gray beasts about it. At sight of the wagon all but one of the six slunk off into the timber. The one stood savagely pat, astride his kill, facing this way with a bare-fanged snarl. "Steady, Benny-boy. It's only a wolf."

Helga had no fear of wolves. Wilderness bred, often through her childhood their howling had sung her to sleep.

But now the other five beasts, encouraged by the one which had stood fast, reappeared in the narrow trail. "Steady there," Helga crooned again. For the wolf smell made both mules skittish. The off-mule wanted to balk and the near-mule to run. “Don’t pay them any mind,” Helga admonished scornfully. “They’re scaredy-cats. Say boo and they run like rabbits.”

Yet when she shouted at them the wolves didn’t run. The six stood aligned across the only aisle of advance, blocking it. There was no way to detour them because the timber on either side was too dense, too cluttered with windfalls and boulders, to permit the passage of a wagon. Helga’s only chance to move on lay in frightening the wolves away.

Today she’d brought no firearm with her. But an axe lay on the narrow footrest she’d made by loading the lower layer of poles a little farther forward than those above. Helga took this axe and stood erect, her right hand brandishing it, her left keeping a grip on the reins. “Get out of my way, you cowards!” she demanded.

Only a yapping of snarls answered her. Their boldness amazed Helga. Usually they went skulking at the sound of a human voice.

Then she remembered something a neighbor had told her last week. That a pack of timber wolves had been raiding sheep down around Del Norte; and that this, plus the fact that a Mexican boy herder had taken to his heels, had emboldened the raiders. It might give them, Helga concluded, a certain contempt of their own for humans.

She kept shouting—but none of the beasts

retreated. Two of them even came closer to the wagon, the other four keeping by the carcass of the doe.

"All right!" Helga challenged. "I'll drive *through* you! Get up, Benny; move along, Buckie." She flapped the reins and Buckie started forward. But Benny, snorting in panic, held back. "Don't let them bluff you, Benny-boy. If you walk right at them they'll scatter like chickens."

She really believed they would. Never had she heard of wolves attacking a driven team. Now she laid aside her axe for the whip. She snapped the whip over Benny so that its tip stung his ear, and he lunged forward. Buckie had been straining to bolt all the while. The brake was now released and there was only one way to go—straight down this narrow lane of tree-walled trail.

Down it, for a few lengths, the wagon rolled; and Helga watched confidently for the wolves to scatter. Then she could drive right over the deer carcass and be on her way.

But ten yards from it the off-mule balked. Helga couldn't force him an inch further. Nor did the wolves scatter. One, the biggest and boldest, edged closer, belly to the snow, and then suddenly leaped in a slashing attack at the off-mule's throat.

Benny squealed, evading the fangs by rearing in harness. Coming down his forelegs straddled a trace chain and it tripped him. He went floundering to his side in the snow, pawing frantically in a tangle of harness.

The other mule kept his feet but stood petrified with terror, anchored by the weight of his mate.

The wolf would leap again, Helga knew, unless she stopped him. She jumped to the ground with the reins in one hand and the axe in the other. A wolf might leap at a mule but he'd never, she was sure, dare leap at an axe-armed human. "Get out!" she screamed. Her left hand dropped the reins and seized the bit ring of Buckie's bridle.

The wolves, like gaunt, brutish statues in the snow, held their line. One was crouched for another spring while the others, back of him, kept guard at the kill. "Away with you!" the girl yelled at them.

Once more the boldest beast leaped forward, fangs snapping, and Helga swung at him with her axe. The mule Buckie reared as she swung, lifting her from her feet and the blade missed. But the rearing of the mule also raised the end of the wagon tongue and its iron-shod point met a shaggy breast. The impact upset the wolf, toppling him belly-up on the snow. Also it jerked the bit ring from Helga's grasp so that her next swing with the axe was two-handed. The blade swished before the wolf could right himself—came down between his eyes and cleaved his skull.

The beast writhed there, pawing the air in

spasms. The off-mule was still down and helpless in a tangle of harness while the near-mule stood anchored by his weight. Helga caught the bit ring again. Amid a chorus of yaps another wolf dashed in; Helga's one-handed swing clipped his foreleg and the wolf, howling, made a limping retreat.

She kept fighting them off, standing ankle-deep in the snow, one hand controlling a panic-stricken team while her other flailed with an axe. Again she crippled a wolf. Then dizziness came over her and she weakened. The long-handled axe with its five-pound head was too heavy. She let go the bridle ring to use both hands. Even then the blade came weakly down; she stood leaning on the axe, gasping for breath.

Then she became aware the battle was over. Two cripples, biting at their wounds, had scuttled into the woods. All except one followed. The one lay dead at her feet.

The girl looked down at the blood-drenched snow. She kept leaning on the axe till a degree of calmness came back. Then she turned to pat Buckie on his soft and still quivering nose. "I told you they're scaredy-cats, didn't I?" To Buckie's mate she said sternly, "You ought to be ashamed of yourself, Benny; acting like that!"

She went back to Benny's singletree and unhooked a trace chain. Next she unhooked the off-neckyoke, slipping the neck-yoke strap from

Benny's collar. This removed all pressure of harness and Helga coaxed Benny to his feet. Him too she gave a pat on the nose. "Don't you worry, Benny-boy; they won't come back."

When she'd straightened out the harness she put a hand on each bridle and backed the wagon half a dozen lengths. There she tethered the team to a sapling. From the tool box she took a hunting knife which was always carried there.

A wolf pelt in winter hair was worth five dollars. The Tarbers were frugal folk and five dollars meant a barrel of flour.

With some revulsion and yet without the slightest hesitation, Helga kneeled in the snow by the wolf. Often she'd helped her father skin a deer. Once she'd helped him strip the pelt from a bear. Now she made five long slits in the hide of a wolf; one down the underbelly from throat to haunch and one the length of each leg.

Soon she had the hide peeled back from a foreleg. It was late afternoon and she'd have to hurry. So Helga worked swiftly, deftly, as sternly self-disciplined as Tarber women had always been. Not that she'd ever known any of them except the mother she'd lost in childhood—her Danish mother who, as an immigrant peasant girl, had met Phineas Tarber on a Boston wharf; and who at Helga's birth a year later had still been able to speak only broken English. Helga could barely remember her. Nor could she remember any of the rugged Tarber women, Vermonters all, among the blood kindred of her father.

Only dimly could she recall the covered wagon in which, at the age of five, she'd traveled from New England to San Luis Park, here in this Colorado wilderness. Since then there'd been hard work aplenty, for man and girl, many a duty tougher than driving a load of poles down a mountain; many a chore rougher and uglier, even, than skinning a wolf.

The skinning of this one was half done when a man's voice startled Helga. She looked up to see a cowboy sitting tall and straight in his saddle. His hat was tipped back, showing hair as black as his eyes, and his lips were quirked in a puzzled smile. Yet something about him told Helga there hadn't been many smiles in his life. Years of knockabout had left marks on his face, for all its youngness. His hands were folded crosswise over the pummel as he looked down at a story printed in the snow.

"How many of 'em were they?" he repeated curiously.

She looked at the brand on his horse. Wagon Wheel. That would be the McCarron outfit, south of Alamosa. The rider stepped down from his saddle and let the reins fall. He came to Helga and took the knife from her. "That's kinda messy work for a girl. I better finish up for you."

He didn't ask it; he simply announced it. He

hunkered by the wolf to resume the skinning. "You better climb back on the wagon," he said matter-of-factly, "before your boots start leakin' water. Snow water leaks mighty bad through boots; a heap worse than rain or creek water."

"It does," Helga agreed, and was frankly grateful. But instead of mounting the wagon she found a seat on a rock by the trail. From there she inspected the stranger's profile and decided he couldn't be much older than herself. He was lean at the face and hips, wide at the shoulders. His belt had a holstered gun. Below the belt were faded denims, skin-tight, and above it he wore a scuffed leather jacket over a checkered shirt.

She remembered his question. "They wouldn't get out of my way," she explained.

"So I notice," he said dryly.

"You ride for the McCarrons?"

He nodded, not looking at her, the job of the moment absorbing him.

"Our place is only a little below here. I'm Helga Tarber."

"I'm Tony Darrow. Strayman for the Wagon Wheel."

She knew that cattle wouldn't range this high in April. But perhaps he was just cutting across from Rock Creek to Del Norte.

"Ain't often they'll bother a team," he remarked, meaning wolves.

She told him the rumor about this particular

pack; how it had devoured sheep and had become bold after the flight of a timid herder.

He went on with the skinning, squatting on his spurs there. “I guess wolves are like some folks I’ve known; let ’em get away with a bluff and first thing you know they’re too big for their britches.”

The air was turning raw and Helga folded her arms, as women will, as a shield against the cold. The quick eyes of Tony Darrow noticed her in that pose and he stopped work for a minute. Long enough to walk to the wagon and take the fleece-lined jacket from the load there. “Better put this on before you get chilled.”

He held the jacket for her, then resumed skinning the wolf. And Helga, sitting on the cold rock, felt pleasantly warm. This was the first time a man had ever held a coat for her.

When the job was done Tony Darrow rolled the pelt into a soggy ball and put it on the wagon. Helga climbed up there and drove on down the trail, the cowboy riding at her wheel.

“You know Margie McCarron?” Helga asked presently. But of course he did. A ranch hand would be sure to know his employer’s daughter; especially when she was a famous beauty and easily the most popular girl in all of San Luis Park. Without waiting for response Helga went on: “I only saw her once. At the Perry House in Alamosa.”

"She'll be there Saturday night," Tony guessed, half to himself.

"At the Perry House? What makes you think so?"

"They're throwin' a fandango there. Never knew Margie to miss one."

Helga looked at him curiously. "Are *you* going?"

"If I get a chance." Riding with a loose-muscled slackness in the saddle, he brought out makings and twisted a cigaret.

"You'll dance with Margie?" Helga prompted.

"If I get a chance." He faced her with a grin that made him look boyish. "They'll be three deep around Margie. They always are."

As the wagon rolled on down the grade, pines gave way to scrub oak and the depth of snow decreased rapidly. Finally they emerged in the open, in the chill of twilight, with all of the park spread out before them.

"She's beautiful, don't you think?" Helga persisted.

"She sure is," Tony agreed. "Purtiest valley in the world, I guess." He waved his hand toward the basin of the Upper Rio Grande, better known as San Luis Park, in a sweep which included everything from Wagon Wheel Gap, to his left, to the New Mexico border at his right. A grassy, sage-streaked plain between high snowy walls, fir-rimmed and sod-floored, the Sangre de

Cristos hugging one side and the San Juans the other. "They tell me she used to be a salty sea but nowadays she's sure a purty cow range."

"I was talking about Margie McCarron."

"She's kinda purty too," Tony admitted.

They came to a wire gate which he opened without dismounting. Helga drove through into a Tarber pasture. A creek meandered across it with a narrow meadow on this side. Its cottonwoods weren't yet in leaf. They stopped at a barn where Phineas Tarber was untracing his plow team.

"This is one of the Wagon Wheel riders, Dad. Tony Darrow."

At once Phineas caught the wolf smell. "What happened, girl?"

Helga jumped to the ground and her laugh had a lilt. "*You* tell him," she said to Tony. "And both of you be ready for supper in an hour."

Tony's eyes followed as she walked with a swinging step, tall and young, to a mud-chinked log house. Then, as he unhitched her team, he described a scene he hadn't witnessed but whose every detail he'd read in the blood-pitted snow.

Phineas, a gaunt, bony man with a granite face, listened imperturbably. "I'll have her take a rifle along," was his only comment, "next trip she makes up the mountain." He led his plow team into the barn and Tony followed with the mules. "The harness goes right there, young man."

When the harness was properly hung and

the teams stalled, Phineas went up into the loft to punch native hay down through traps above each manger. Tony brought his saddle mount in and soon all five animals were feeding. “Better stretch it, hadn’t we?” he suggested as Tarber took the wolf hide from the wagon.

They carried the hide to the outer south wall of the barn where it would get the most sun. Soon they had it spread and tacked there.

“I’ll fill the trough,” Tony offered, moving to a pulley well in the barnyard. A hollowed half log made a trough and Tony, drawing bucket after oaken bucket, filled it to the brim. The horses and mules, having by then fed and cooled a little, were led out to water. “What next?” the cowboy asked. A man like Phineas Tarber would never go to supper till the last chore was done.

So they unloaded the wagon by fast-fading light, stacking the poles atop others which Helga had earlier hauled down the mountain.

As dark came on, Phineas lighted a lantern. He led Tony to a bench back of the house. A pail, washpan and soap were there. The kitchen door opened and Helga appeared in a skirt and blouse. A starched yellow apron matched the coiled braids of her hair. Tony became aware for the first time that she was good to look at. Not small and dainty and gorgeously red-haired, like Margie McCarron, but still she was nice for a man to look at. “You’ll need this,” Helga said, smiling as she handed out a kettle of hot water.

Tony took off his shirt, soaped his arms and face. When he was rid of the wolf taint he brushed his hair, a little more carefully than usual, by a mirror which hung over the bench.

In the kitchen a table was set for three. Phineas Tarber, a Puritan of ten generations, said grace. Helga served them with side meat and hominy.

Furnishings in sight were simple, severe, scrupulously useful. None of the fluffy frills with which Margie McCarron embellished the Wagon Wheel house. Here in the Tarber kitchen Tony noticed a shelf of books, most of them textbooks ranging from primers to an algebra. Helga saw his eye on them and explained: "This country had no schools when we came here. Dad taught me till I was thirteen; then I went to school at Del Norte."

"That," Tony said, "is more schoolin' than I ever had."

"You were raised here in the park?"

"No. On a farm in Indiana."

"Didn't they have good schools there?"

A strange impulse took hold of Tony. He looked into this girl's friendly eyes and wanted to tell her what he'd never told before. Something which had been locked tightly inside of him since his twelfth year. Why he should want to reveal it now, to these strangers, he couldn't analyze. Perhaps it was because he sensed he could tell it for the first time to sympathetic ears. For a thread in this girl's background seemed to parallel one in his own; at least Helga Tarber, like himself, had missed out on the fun of a childhood schoolground.

"My folks died when I was six," Tony told her, his black eyes narrow and far away with the memory, "and they bound me out to a farmer—apprenticed is the right word, I guess. The agreement said I was to have three months' schooling each winter till I was eighteen, and when I was twenty-one I was to get a horse and saddle."

Helga looked at him with shocked eyes. "You mean it's still legal to do that? In a free country?"

"It was in Indiana," Tony assured her, "when I was a kid. This man I was bound out to was a skinflint. He worked me seven days a week sunup to sundown. I got three months' schooling of winters, all right, but the schoolhouse was right across the road so I ate lunch at home. Always I had to do chores till the bell rang. Same before and after school, so I never got a chance to play with the other kids."

"And all the pay you were to get for this," Helga protested, "was the promise of a horse and saddle when you were twenty-one?"

Tony looked at her and grinned. "That was the deal. But the contract didn't say what *kind* of a horse and saddle. And purty soon I knew it would be a crowbait, spavined and cheap-saddled. He was that kind of a skinner, this farmer . . . So when I was twelve years old I lit out. Put some cold muffins in my pocket and started runnin' down the road."

2

Although Helga urged him to tell more, he cut the tale short right there. A reaction of shyness came over Tony, a sense of shame for having bared even that much of his life. Presently he stood up and reached for his hat.

"I'll be joggin' on down to Del Norte now. I sure thank you folks for a nice feed."

Phineas Tarber nodded toward a trap in the ceiling. "We've a cot in the loft," he invited. "Glad to have you stay all night."

"No use in it," Tony said. "It's only six miles to Del Norte."

Phineas lighted him to the barn with a lantern. Helga waved a goodbye. "Don't let the wolves get you," Tony called back to her.

Shortly he was riding down a trail to Del Norte. Looping a leg around the saddle horn, he let the horse walk while he rolled a smoke. Creek cottonwoods reared naked arms in the starlight. "She's got nerve to burn!" Tony marveled. "But it's not right to work a girl that hard. Wonder how she'd handle herself at a *baile*."

Two cigarets later he'd brushed Helga Tarber from his mind and was thinking ahead to Saturday—and a *baile* at Alamosa—and red-haired Margie McCarron.

Riding into Del Norte he found it unnaturally quiet. Unsaddling at the livery barn Tony mentioned this to the hostler. "It's that danged boom they got on down at Alamosa," the barnman explained. "Lots o' folks are pullin' up stakes and movin' down there. They say we're even gonna lose our bank. Grain him, mister?"

"Not till morning. A forkful of hay'll do right now."

Tony went down the plank walk to a hotel. "Sure we got a vacant bed," the proprietor said gloomily. "We ain't had much of anything else since the railroad built into Alamosa."

Pulling off his boots upstairs Tony recalled his last visit to Del Norte. Then it had been the metropolis of the park. In fact the town was a thriving trade center long before Alamosa was anything but a patch of sagebrush on the bank of the Rio Grande. But in July of '78 the narrow gauge of the D & RG, having traversed Le Veta Pass, had arrived at Alamosa; and from there it was building on toward Cumbres Pass and Durango, missing Del Norte a cool thirty miles.

Tony blew out his lamp and crawled into bed. No wonder the merchants here were disgruntled. But the United States Land Office was still at Del Norte. Which reminded Tony of his own errand. Why, he wondered, had Receiver Halderman of the land office sent for him?

• • •

In the morning he went to find out. But Guy Halderman wasn't at his office. "He's in town, though," a clerk said. "Come back in a couple of hours."

Strolling up the sidewalk Tony found a knot of citizens in front of the bank. A notice on the door said:

> This bank will close business here at noon Friday April 30th and will reopen at 9.00 A. M. Monday May 3rd at the northeast corner of Front Street and Hunt Avenue in Alamosa. All accounts will be protected and the continued patronage of depositors is cordially invited.
>
> J. L. MCNEIL, Vice-Pres.

"Leavin' us high and dry," a bystander muttered. "Means I'll have to ride thirty mile every time I wanta cash a check."

"Don't reckon we can blame Mac any," another put in. "He does business all over southwest Colorado—Silverton, Lake City, Pagosa Springs, Parrot City, Ouray—so he might as well do it from Alamosa as here, seein' as Alamosa's got the track and we ain't."

Tony went on to the livery barn for a look at his horse. Teamsters there were preparing two stout wagons for the move. Today was April thirtieth, so at noon they'd begin loading the bank's counters, partitions, furniture, safe, books, everything.

Guy Halderman was at his desk when Tony returned to the land office. The receiver was a small gray man with an earnest voice and honest brown eyes. Having never seen him before, Tony was astonished when the man offered him a job. The pay mentioned was twice the pay of a ranch strayman.

"But you don't even know me, Mr. Halderman!"

The receiver smiled gravely as he looked Tony over from head to spurs. "I know a top hand when I see one. I asked Alva Adams to recommend me a top hand and he named you, Darrow."

Alva Adams ran the leading hardware store at Alamosa. He was a big name in the park, up to his neck in politics and already being mentioned as a candidate for governor. Tony had met Alva through the man's young brother Billy, a popular rangeman well known and welcome at every ranch in the park.

"Before I tell you what this job is," Halderman began in a tone of confidence, "you must promise to forget it in case you'd rather not accept. It's undercover work, you understand."

"I won't mention it to anybody," Tony agreed. "What kind of undercover work is it?"

Halderman led him to the open door and waved a hand toward the vast reaches of the park. "A hundred thousand quarter-section homesteads lie out there. And an army of homeseekers is wheeling west to file them. We want them to come. The country needs them. That's why we passed the Homestead Act of '62. It's good land and it's free land. It's empty land waiting for land-hungry men."

"It sure is," Tony agreed.

The man's earnest voice went on: "Every mail brings me new filings. Most of them are honest, but a few are fraudulent. When we get proof of fraud we cancel the filing and restore the land to the public domain. Trouble is we only have time and personnel to check on about one in every ten filings. So thousands of acres have been patented illegally."

"How do they work it, Mr. Halderman?"

The receiver took him back to the desk and picked up a homestead application at random. "Chances are this one's all right. You notice the filing fee of sixteen dollars is pinned to it. A ten, a five and a one-dollar bill. Applicant named Juan Baca. It's a quarter section more than a hundred miles west of here. Everything seems to be on the level. Three years from now the government will probably issue Juan Baca a patent deed to the land."

The application, Tony saw, was on the proper land office form and had been signed before the clerk of the county court of La Plata County, at

Parrot City, Colorado. A printed instruction on the form said that both application and final proof paper had to be signed before an officer either of a county court or of the U. S. Land Department.

"Suppose some rancher over that way," Halderman suggested with troubled eyes, "has a hay hand named Juan Baca. 'Juan,' he says, 'I need another quarter section to square out my east pasture. I've filled in a homestead form to cover it. Take it to the courthouse and sign it before the clerk of the court—and keep your mouth shut. I'll pin on the fee and mail it in. Three years from now there'll be another paper for you to sign the same way. When they issue you a patent, convey it to me. Meantime you can always count on a job here, Juan. By the way, here's a little present for your wife.' "

Tony stared. "You mean he could get away with that?"

"Land hogs are getting away with it, wholesale, all over the west. How do you suppose some of these big ranches grow so fast?"

"Why don't you crack down on it, Mr. Halderman?"

"Intend to. But I can't revoke a filing without evidence of fraud. That's where you'd come in."

"How?"

"By working first at one ranch, then at another, with your eyes and ears open. When you get wind of a rancher using the name of a pawn for a land filing, report it and I'll do the rest."

"You want me to be a spy!" Tony summed up bluntly.

"Call it that if you want. It's a kind of secret government service."

Tony didn't like it. He thought of his present situation at the McCarron place, where they treated him almost like one of the family. It would be the same on any other ranch. "You want me to take bed and board from a cowman, ride his horses, and then tell tales on him?"

"If there are tales to tell, yes."

"No thanks." Tony hated to say it, because he liked this small gray man with the earnest voice and honest brown eyes. "I'm just not cut out for a snooping job like that."

Halderman looked deeply disappointed. "Sorry you feel that way. You promised not to mention it, remember?"

"I won't tell anybody," Tony promised again.

His eyes veered to a huge map on the wall. It was a government map showing all the public lands under the jurisdiction of this office. Black dots marked homestead filings, but far more than ninety percent of the map was still white.

A slow smile crept up Tony's face as he fished a slip of paper from his pocket. "Last coupla months," he confided, "I've kinda had the homesteading itch myself. Figure I could spend six months a year proving up and the other six months riding for some ranch."

Halderman nodded. "Many a ranch hand has started his own outfit that way."

"Is this piece still vacant?" Tony exposed his slip on which was scribbled a quarter description, by section, township and range.

The receiver looked at it, crossed the room, consulted his master map, then turned with a smile. "It's wide open, Darrow. A bottomland quarter on the Conejos River, about two miles above the old Zebulon Pike stockade."

"I camped there a few times," Tony said. "Grass stirrup-high and a nice cottonwood grove on the river." His eyes narrowed. "I've half a notion to dab down on it."

"No reason you can't," Halderman said heartily, "if you're twenty-one years old and own no other land. If you like I'll have a clerk fill out the form for you."

Tony took sixteen dollars from his wallet. "Here's your filing fee." He grinned. "I'm stakin' that claim right now."

When the application was filled out Receiver Halderman personally acknowledged his signature. "You get possession at once, you understand. But you won't get a title until you send in your proof paper three years from now."

On his way to the livery barn, to saddle up for Alamosa, Tony stopped at a restaurant for a cup of coffee. It was across the street from the bank before which two stout wagons were drawn up.

"You're just the bird I'm lookin' for, kiddo. How you doin'?"

The voice had an oily slyness and the face, as Tony turned toward it, seemed unpleasantly familiar. The man had rounded shoulders and a straw-yellow skin. His eyes and nose were too small for the beefiness of his build. His visored cap and his lack of sunburn meant he wasn't a rangeman. Without invitation he slipped into a seat opposite Tony. "Don't tell me you don't know me, kiddo." The sly lips took a twist. "Your old cellmate, Lew Wager?"

Wager! The shock of him, to Tony Darrow, was like an iron fist.

The man dropped a lid over one of his shifty, undersized eyes. "Whatcha doin', kiddo?"

A million bitter memories came crowding back and a tightness in Tony's throat made it hard to answer Lew Wager. "I'm strayman," he managed to say, "for the Wagon Wheel ranch."

"How much you make?"

"Thirty and found, if it's any of your business. What the devil are *you* doing this far west, Wager?"

Again the eyelid drooped. "Lookin' for a quick way to get rich—and I've just found it. All I need is a good man like you to help."

"Help you do what?"

"See that bank over there? It's loadin' everything it's got, includin' forty thousand in gold coin, on them wagons. And tomorrow they drive thirty miles to Alamosa. A driver and one shotgun guard on each wagon."

"And you want me to help you stick 'em up?"

"Why not? We can mask up, can't we? And bury the coin in a sand dune somewhere."

Tony fought away an impulse to swing a punch. "Get out of here," he said quietly. "Get out before I twist your neck."

Wager appeared surprised rather than resentful. "So that's it? Goin' straight, huh?"

"I never went any other way. Now hike."

Wager shrugged his big, curved shoulders and stood up. "Okay, kiddo. If that's the way you feel about it." He slouched a step toward the exit and then came back. The flush of a threat rode his face. "You won't mention this little idea o' mine, naturally. I mean you won't be passin' no tip to the sheriffs."

"What makes you think I won't?"

Again Wager's lips took a crafty twist. "Because they'd wanta know how I happened to spring it on you. A guy don't spring a deal like that on no stranger. But you ain't no stranger, kiddo. And they's records in the Jeff City pen to prove it. You wouldn't want folks to find out about it, wouldja? Nice ranchfolks like where you work, maybe?"

Wager sauntered out and turned toward the nearest saloon.

Tony was too shaken to finish his coffee. He went out with the intention of hunting up the law. Yet discretion stopped him in his tracks. Wager was right. Exposing the man's proposal would expose Tony's own record.

It would cost him, for one thing, his job at the Wagon Wheel. Mark McCarron wasn't likely to keep an ex-convict on his payroll.

A stinging frustration gripped Tony. He'd wanted to tell the McCarrons. He'd dreaded for them to hear about it from any other lips than his own. Yet now he didn't dare. He'd waited too long. He didn't dare tell—until he found a man called Memphis Jack. What the rest of his name was Tony didn't know. Memphis Jack Somebody, an itinerant Tennessee farm hand. He alone, of all the world, knew Tony was innocent of the thing for which he'd been judged guilty.

Now he had the bitter sense of being right back where he'd started. Standing helplessly before a Missouri jury who wouldn't believe him. A boy alone without a shred of proof, facing a hostile courtroom. And only the nondescript Memphis Jack could have helped him.

After serving his term Tony had hunted high and low for the man, learning finally that he'd last been heard of at Alamosa, Colorado. So Tony himself had come hotfoot to this range, hoping to find a witness to his innocence, finding instead a new life at the Wagon Wheel ranch.

I've still got to find him, Tony thought wretchedly. *I'll never ride easy till I do.* And until he did he must keep the secret of his past.

Yet Wager was a fact and had to be dealt with. Tony went to the livery barn and found a hostler cleaning out stalls. "Did a fella named Wager leave his bronc here?"

The man nodded. "That roan back there?"

The roan's stall had a rack with a saddle draped over it. A repeating carbine was in the saddle boot. Over the horn hung a belt weighted with a forty-five gun.

Which meant Wager was equipped with the tools of his trade. Maybe he'd find someone else to help him hold up the bank wagons!

It was a challenge on which Tony couldn't turn his back. Instead of riding on to Alamosa, he must keep an eye on Wager. What was the man doing now?

Tony went up the street and looked in the saloon he'd seen Wager enter. Wager wasn't there. Two miners were tossing dice. Others at the bar were gunslung drifters. Off-scourings of the ranges—frontier towns were cursed with them and Del Norte was no exception. Wager would have all day—and a wide choice of talent—to pick a partner for his crime.

In a second saloon Tony found similar customers, but again Wager wasn't among them. He made every dive on the street and failed to locate the man.

It was now well past noon and the bank had begun the business of moving. Men were bringing out desks and chairs to load them on two wagons. Others were dismantling the tellers' cages and tearing down partitions. Curious townsfolk watched from the street. From a hum of talk Tony knew that the program of moving was no secret. Everything would be loaded by sundown. The wagons would then be driven into a private barn and held under lock for the night. Tomorrow they'd be driven thirty miles to Alamosa.

A driver and a shotgun-armed companion would be on each wagon seat. Who, Tony asked, would be the shotgun-armed companions?

"Mac himself'll be on one wagon. And Alf Camp on the other."

Tony's uneasiness grew. A banker with a shotgun across his knees, plus a driver busy holding reins, could be setups for a pair of bandits shooting from ambush with repeating rifles. The wagon crews could be riddled before an answering shot was fired.

All risk would be avoided if Tony gave warning in advance. But if he did Wager would tell a tale himself!

Tony went back to the livery barn. Wager's roan was still there. But the racked saddle seemed a bit bulkier than before. Saddlebags which had been flat now had bulges. "Wager been here, last hour or so?"

"He stopped by with another guy," the hostler said. "Just wanted to see if I'd fed his bronc."

Tony's hand made quick delves into the roan's saddlebags to see what had been added within the hour. Two stout grain sacks and a pair of black handkerchiefs!

Masks and loot bags! Wager must have recruited a helper.

It was late afternoon before Tony located them. He spotted them at a hardware counter buying ammunition. Wager and a long, lean man with a tough, cleft chin. As the pair came out Tony screened himself back of a freight wagon.

When they were out of hearing he said to the wagoneer: "That's Pete Hicks, ain't it? I mean the skinny guy with Lew Wager."

The wagoneer looked up the walk. "Nope. He's Frank Tully. Used to deal faro up at Saguache but they run him outa town."

As the pair turned a corner, Tony followed. Warily he trailed them to a back-street cantina. Tully had a horse tied in front of it and the saddle boot had a rifle. The pair stopped at the tie rack long enough to stow the purchased ammunition into saddlebags. After which they went into the cantina.

Passing by, Tony shot a quick glance inside.

Wager and Tully were at a table, whispering. Tully's was a stupid face, Tony thought, stupid but evil and dangerous. Wager had the look of a schemer, Tully the look of a killer. The look of a man born to hang, and who until then would kill and rob and run.

3

Tony waited till dark before riding out of town. He took the Alamosa stage road down the right bank of the Rio Grande.

Later tonight Tully and Wager would take this same trail. They'd pick their spot of ambush and be ready when the wagons came along.

The river cottonwoods were on Tony's left, while to his right lay open sage. Black sage and the strong tang of it filled his nostrils. Maybe the outlaws would attack from the river brush; or maybe they'd pick some dry arroyo further on.

About three miles out of town a cottonwood grove had an undergrowth of wild plum. Back of it lay the trough of the river, its riffles faintly audible from the road. Tony turned in there and rode his horse down a bank to a gravel shoal. Turning some fifty yards downstream he picketed the horse under a brushy bluff.

He unstrapped a slicker roll from the saddle's cantle and from this took his extra gun. The habitual wearing of two guns was, to Tony Darrow, a thing unbecoming to a workaday cowboy. Show-off toughies often did it, but not men who worked stock for a living. Yet sometimes an emergency came along where a second gun could be handy; so Tony had put one in his saddle roll.

Now he wedged it into his belt and climbed the bank. With little branches slapping his face spitefully, he groped his way back to the road. A nearly full moon was up, just topping the Sangre de Cristos. He'd need a little light when he stopped Tully and Wager.

Complete surprise would be his advantage. They'd be covered before they knew he was here. The idea was to unhorse and disarm them. On foot and gunless they could be left to their own devices.

Their planned ambush was probably much further on than this. But to get there they must ride by this spot.

An hour passed and no one came by. Then Tony heard hoofbeats. He crouched in the brush with a gun in each hand. But it was only the Lake City to Alamosa stage. The big Barlow and Sanderson carrier, drawn by four horses, went rumbling by. It had come through Wagon Wheel Gap and was heading for the railroad at Alamosa.

A long wait later, a buckboard rattled by, pulled by matched trotters. By his profile Tony recognized the driver—Oscar Wilkins of Alamosa. A shaggy bearskin coat enveloped the man and Tony, as the chill of night grew, wished he had one like it.

At about midnight two ranch riders passed, heading for Del Norte. One was humming a tune and the other seemed half asleep in his saddle.

The moon rode at zenith. Tony, chafing his hands, tramped about the grove to keep up circulation. Overhead he heard a clawing on bark, perhaps a restless raccoon. Back of him the Rio Grande murmured in unceasing riffles.

He'd be in no shape, Tony thought, for tomorrow night's shindig at the Perry House. He'd counted on seeing Margie there. Now an odd thought struck him. During all the year he'd known Margie he hadn't dared confide to her any part of his background. And yet after knowing that other girl barely two hours—what was her name, Helga Tarber?—he'd blabbed it out. What did *she* think of him? What would she think if she knew he'd been tried and convicted, at the age of eighteen, of stealing horses?

It lacked only an hour of daylight when he heard them coming. Two horsemen jogging down the road. Peering out Tony saw them riding stirrup to stirrup. Wager was on the side nearest him. The other horse was black, and the man astride of it was long and lean enough to be Tully.

Tony cocked both guns. Tully might make a fight of it. Wager was a canny schemer, Tully a loose-triggered killer.

Wager's voice floated down the night. "Pass me the makings, fella."

The lean man passed a tobacco sack and they slowed to a walk while Wager built a cigaret. It was a better break than Tony had hoped for. He stepped out in front of them. “Reach, Tully.” He aimed a gun at each rider.

Wager, spilling his smoke, reached high. Tully went for his gun.

The one in Tony’s left hand blazed. Its bullet rang against the steel of Tully’s half-drawn forty-five. “Yeow!” The shriek was Tully’s as his gun dropped to the road.

Twice more Tony fired and the San Juans threw back echoes. One of the shots tickled Wager’s ear and the other punctured Tully’s high, peaked hat. “Just in case you think I’m fooling.”

Panic contorted the heavy, small-eyed face of Wager. He’d exchanged his visored cap for a slouch felt. “What’s the idea, sheriff?” Tully’s voice came in a croaking falsetto. “We was just ridin’ down the road mindin’ our business.”

Tony advanced and took Wager’s gun. “Step down, both of you.”

When they were unhorsed he made them lie face-down in the road. He hung their holster guns on the saddle horns. “What made you think I was a sheriff, Tully?”

Wager warned weakly, “You’ll be sorry.”

“I’d be still sorrier if I’d let you hold up those bank wagons.” One of the saddles had a pair of pigging strings. Tony used one to hobble Tully and the other to hobble Wager. “Just so you can’t run away,” he explained, “while we take a walk.”

He got them to their feet and made them hobble

ahead of him through the grove. In the gloom they might have made a dash for it had their ankles been free. At the river bed Tony prodded them down the shoal to his own tethered mount.

"I'll leave your broncs and your hardware," he promised them, "at the depot tie rack in Alamosa. So long."

He stepped into his saddle and spurred to the road level. "You'll be sorry." Wager's threat followed him hoarsely from the river.

It would take them a few minutes, Tony estimated, to get untied. Then they could either walk or beg a ride from some wagoneer.

He linked the roan and the black at the end of a lead rope and led them as he moved on at a trot toward Alamosa. Shortly the road turned left and forded the Rio Grande. It continued down the other bank and came presently to a cluster of adobe shacks known as Seven Mile Plaza. No sign of life was there, not even a barking dog.

Ten miles out of Del Norte a roadside ranch appeared in the lonely dawnlight. Here a chimney showed smoke and a corral had horses in it. This was known as Venable's Station and the stage always changed horses here. Tony rode on without stopping.

Two hours and ten more miles took him to Spalding's ranch, another change station for the daily stage. Ten miles was as far as horses could normally trot, pulling a coach.

The sun was now peeping past Mount Blanca. And just to the left of Blanca, at the foot of Mosca Pass, towering reddish lumps reared weirdly from the sage-black floor of the valley. The Great Singing Sand Dunes, men called them—naked, barren, mysterious, forever changing color with each new angle of the sun, and forever whispering with the sighs of shifting sands. Sight of them now, as always, laid a soothing hand on Tony Darrow. Always their bigness had made his own worries seem small.

In midmorning he recrossed the river at Alamosa. Dust made a powdery footing along Fifth Street as he followed it to Hunt Avenue. Stores along here were frame or adobe, unpainted and false-fronted. A Saturday crowd was in town and the tie racks were full. Ranch teams, hitched in harness to endgates, munched hay from wagon beds. Raised board sidewalks swarmed with the busy and the idle.

Leading two saddled horses Tony turned left on Hunt and rode to Front Street, which paralleled the narrow-gauge tracks. He got rid of the led horses by tying them to the depot rack. Each captive mount still had a rifle in the saddle scabbard and a six-gun hanging from the horn.

Tony smiled wearily. If Wager and Tully had caught a ride on some downriver wagon, they might not be far behind him.

Tony led his own mount across Front to the

Victoria Hotel. "Want me to stable him for you, mister?" A hotel boy was on the walk and Tony tossed him the reins. "Sure, Eddie, and here's two-bits. Say, I notice they've slicked up that empty building across the way."

"It's gonna be the new bank, mister. Folks say it's movin' down from Del Norte right now. Have you seen Mr. Amory's fancy stallion? He's showin' it off up on State Avenue."

"Not yet, Eddie." Tony went in and registered. The clerk gave him room twelve.

"I checked a bag here last time I was in town. Send it up, please." Like many ranch workers Tony commonly kept a bag at his favorite hotel, to avoid packing one back and forth asaddle.

Before going up, he decided to walk a block west to the Perry House and get a ticket for tonight's party there.

Hunt to State, along Front, was the town's busiest block. Today its sidewalk swarmed with rangemen and railroaders. Midway along it Tony passed the big Adams hardware establishment. He moved on to Slavick's saloon on the State corner. A canvas-covered wagon was watering its bullock team at a public trough in front of Slavick's; and directly across State from this, on an upper balcony of the Perry House, a bevy of ranch girls stood watching a performance in the street.

From a sidewalk crowd, applause crackled

as though a parade were passing. The parade consisted of but one man and his horse. Blaise Amory on an Arabian stallion. A big proud sorrel with a flashing golden tail and mane to match. Blaise was putting him through the fancy paces which had won a blue ribbon at a recent Denver horse show. “Ride him pretty, Blaise!” the crowd yelled.

Blaise Amory was, Tony observed, himself no less showy than his mount. His was the tallest, creamiest Stetson in town. Gilt fretwork adorned his elbow-length wrist guards and his vest had braid on it. The man held the reins chin-high while with coaxing commands and subtle knee pressures he made the stallion prance, dance, mince, all but cakewalk down the middle of the street.

Watching him made Tony conscious of his own shabbiness. He’d lost a night’s sleep and was saddle weary. He saw Blaise Amory wheel to a stop in front of the Perry House, take off his hat and wave a salute to a balcony audience.

They were ranch girls in for tonight’s dance—a huddle of flounced skirts and curls and rosy cheeks. Among them Tony spied Margie McCarron, the prettiest of them all, a bonnet over her brilliant red bangs and tied with a ribbon under her chin. Now as always she quickened Tony’s pulse a little. But he was glad she didn’t see him and the twenty-eight-hour stubble on his face. She was bending over the balcony rail and calling down, “Make him kneel, Blaise.”

“I’ll kneel to you myself, Margie,” Blaise shouted gallantly, “any time you say so.”

As the man made his mount kneel before beauty, Tony noticed the dagger-sharp rowels of his spurs and the heavy, punishing Spanish bit on the bridle. Blaise used them, no doubt, to discipline and train the stallion. A thought came to Tony that only a man with something basically cruel in his character would use a bit and spurs like those.

Now he elbowed his way through the crowd and into the Perry House lobby. After picking up a ticket for tonight he hurried back to the Victoria. He paused at the desk there to ask that hot water be sent up to his room. A middle-aged Mexican was accosting the clerk and his brown, pocked face looked a bit sullen. “Yes, Pancho,” the clerk was saying, “Mr. Amory has a room here. Number seven. But he’s out just now.”

Tony went up to room twelve and found his bag there. When the hot water came he took a sponge bath. After a shave and a change his spirits were high again. He forgot the threat of Lew Wager. Today was today and tonight he’d be waltzing with Margie McCarron.

Now he stretched on the bed and slept.

When he awoke it lacked less than an hour of dark. His first thought was: had the bank wagons arrived from Del Norte? To find out Tony started down to the lobby. In the upper hall he met Blaise Amory.

"Hi, neighbor!" Amory gave him a slap on his back. He was always hearty that way. But sometimes a wee bit condescending, Tony thought, toward payroll cow hands. Amory, of course, had a ranch and a payroll of his own. "Been out riding for strays, I suppose? Run into any of my Jaybird stuff?"

"What few I saw were doing all right," Tony said.

"Thanks, neighbor." Amory's was a handsome, ever-smiling face, burnished a golden brown and set with bright blue eyes, his hair wavy and as blond as the mane of his stallion. "See you at the hop tonight." Again a slap on Tony's shoulder, after which the man turned into room seven.

Maybe I'm just jealous! Tony brooded as he went on downstairs. Or was there some other reason why he'd never liked Blaise Amory? The man had a wide popularity in the park. *But he just can't help showing off! 'Specially when there's womenfolks around!*

In the lobby Tony bought a current issue of the *Alamosa Weekly Independent* and settled down at a front window. Looking out across Hunt, he knew the bank wagons hadn't arrived. Otherwise they'd be drawn up in front of the new quarters over there.

Looking obliquely across Front, he could see the depot. The two saddled horses he'd left at the tie rack were gone. Which meant Tully and Wager had arrived to reclaim them. They'd be plenty sore, Tony reasoned. But he shrugged them off.

Skimming through the *Independent*, Tony learned that Company A of the 22nd Infantry was now on duty at Fort Garland; that a drama called *Dora* was to be staged at the Alamosa Opera House; that a strike at Conejos Camp was showing "fifty colors to the pan"; and that one E. L. Vancel had just purchased Theodore Emperius's cub bear for fifty dollars, and would fight her against a bulldog for a side bet of a thousand.

On the editorial page Tony read a bitter complaint that the "riffraff and the lawless" had followed the railroad into Alamosa and were giving the town a bad name; that cowboys from the ranches, miners from Summitville and soldiers from Fort Garland were flocking in for orgies of dissipation.

Another editorial caught Tony's eye:

> Our Denver correspondent assures us that our leading merchant and distinguished fellow townsman, Alva Adams, now serving us so well in the state legislature, has a fair chance for his party's

> nomination for governor. The *Independent* is willing to go much further than that. We hereby predict that Alva will not only be nominated but elected, and that he will serve Colorado with distinction. Nor will we be much surprised if that kid brother of his, Billy Adams, should also make a name for himself some day.

Wheels creaking down Hunt drew Tony's attention. He looked out and saw the two bank wagons arriving from Del Norte. From the opposite direction a clanging bell announced an incoming train. Which meant that a swarm of passengers would be rushing over here for supper. To get ready for it himself Tony hurried back up to his room.

In the upper hall a Mexican was knocking at the door of room seven. Tony recognized the same sullen peon who'd inquired at the desk for Blaise Amory. Tony turned into his own room and as he began rubbing up his boots he became aware that a knocking down the hall continued. A voice reached him from just outside room seven. "Señor Amory! It is I, Pancho Morales. May I speak with you, *si gusta*?"

No answer came from the room's inmate. After a while the knocker gave up and went down the stairs. But why, Tony wondered, hadn't Amory admitted him? Amory was in there for Tony had seen him enter. Nor could he have gone out again without passing Tony in the lobby.

It didn't seem important. Tony brushed it from his mind.

Nor did the incident at once recur to Tony when, two hours later, he again strolled a block west up Front Street. The sidewalk was lighted, this noisy Saturday night, only by a full moon and glows from the saloons. Piano music rattled from Slavick's as Tony reached the corner of State Avenue.

Across it the Perry House was swarming with gay guests. Ed Murdy of the Jaybird saw Tony. "Hurry up, fella," Murdy yelled. "You're late." Tony saw Abundo Martinez, from Conejos, arrive and hand his two handsome daughters to the walk. Up the Perry House steps they went in a rustling of silks.

Tony was heading that way himself when he saw Pancho Morales. Morales sat on the stoop of the town marshal's office, two doors up State, in a pose of waiting. This office was locked and dark. But every other window in the block was lighted. O'Brien's Oyster House, next to it, had every table filled.

When the gunshot came Tony at first assumed it was some Saturday night celebrant sounding off. He knew better when he saw Pancho Morales topple forward on the walk.

A young girl, crossing toward the Perry House

on her escort's arm, gave a half-smothered scream. A dozen men closed in on Pancho Morales. One of them, a druggist, kneeled by the fallen man. Presently he reported: "The man's dead. Better get Milt here right away."

4

Milt Yeager was marshal of Alamosa and an undersheriff of Conejos County. His questions detained Tony Darrow, as a witness, and made Tony hours late at the dance.

Fifty couples were whirling about the Perry House dining room. Most of them hadn't yet heard about a killing in the street. On a raised platform John Moomaw's five-piece orchestra was whipping out a fast tempo waltz. Simon Frank's violin was singing while Banjo Joe thumped away with thumb and boot.

At once Tony circled for a glimpse of Margie McCarron.

She was slighter in figure than other girls on the floor and it was a moment before he saw her. She was dancing with Blaise Amory, her flaming crown of hair reaching barely to his shoulder. Tony held up an eager hand as they passed. "Next is mine, Margie?"

She smiled, shook her head and was lost among the gliding couples.

"She had a full card, last I saw of it." The voice came from Tony's elbow. "You should've been here on time, like Blaise was."

Tony turned to his stockily built employer, Mark McCarron. "A shooting across the street.

I happened to see it and Milt Yeager had a few questions."

"Who did it?" McCarron took an unlighted cigar from his mouth. Except for his sky-blue eyes he didn't look at all like Margie. His plump face had color, like Margie's, but in the father's case it came from rich living and liquor. He wasn't a hard-riding rangeman, yet no ranch in the park was operated more shrewdly than the Wagon Wheel.

"Nobody knows," Tony said. "Sounded like the shot came from back of a boxcar on a siding across Front. Rifle shot."

"Who got shot?" McCarron put the cold cigar back between his teeth. Short and solid, he had to look up at Tony.

"Fella named Pancho Morales. 'Scuse me, Mr. McCarron."

The music had stopped and Tony made a dash for Margie. She was in midfloor with Blaise Amory, Amory's hands popping to promote an encore. "I thought you weren't coming, Tony. So I haven't a dance left." Margie's tone implied that it was a major calamity not only for Tony but for herself. She gave him one of her most radiant smiles. "Not a single one. Look." The girl held up her dance card to prove it.

In dismay Tony saw that every dance was taken; also that Blaise Amory's name was on every fourth line. He let out a howl. "What's the idea letting Blaise crowd out the homefolks, Margie? I'm a loyal Wagon Wheeler, ain't I? Divvy up, fella."

Amory waved him away. "Chase yourself, strayman." He stood there like a great golden god slanting a smile of dismissal at Tony, then turned to look fondly and possessively at Margie McCarron.

"Where've you been all week, Tony?" she demanded.

"I been rescuin' a beautiful lady," Tony said cunningly, "from a pack of wolves."

"You haven't any such thing." She looked up curiously at him, adding quickly; "Where? Who is she?"

"It's such a long yarn, Margie, that it'd take me a whole dance to tell about it. Now if this tight-fisted Jaybirder'd loosen up on one . . ."

"You're not going to be a pig, are you, Blaise?" Margie turned coaxingly with just the hint of a calculated pout which no man in the park had yet been able to resist. "He can have just one, can't he, Blaise?"

"Just one." Amory gave a grudging shrug of surrender. "And that's more'n you rate, stray-man." He took the card, erased his own name after number fifteen and jotted Tony's there.

The Moomaw and his musicians crashed into an encore. Amory's braided sleeve encircled Margie and they whirled away.

Dance number fifteen was more than an hour off and Tony was in no mood for a partner other than Margie. He went out into the lobby and stood at a street window. On the opposite walk Milt Yeager was still questioning witnesses. Morales' body had been taken away. It would be morning before a coroner could arrive from Conejos and conduct an inquest.

Two men emerged from Slavick's saloon and Tony recognized the frustrated bandits, Wager and Tully. They were in some sharp disagreement. Standing just outside Slavick's lighted doorway, arguing, each in turn shook his head as the other spoke. Presently they parted and disappeared in opposite directions.

Tony went back to the dance floor where Margie was still dancing with Amory. Mark McCarron, cigar upturned obliquely from his lips, stood watching the couple. The man's expression of paternal approval depressed Tony. For the first time it occurred to him that McCarron was on Amory's side in the race of a dozen young men who were buzzing about Margie.

Nor could McCarron be blamed, Tony thought gloomily. Amory had a ranch and a ditch right, a cow brand and a cavvy of mounts. Also he'd picked up odd bits of real estate all over the park, and had a reputation as a shrewd speculator. All of it gave him stature, just like that big sorrel stallion with a mane to match his own golden hair.

From another direction Tony heard his name called. Simon Frank was beckoning from the platform. Tony shook his head but it was no use. Simon walked across the room to hand Tony his fiddle and bow. "I'm tuckered out, cowboy. Spell me a bit."

Off the man went toward the nearest bar, leaving Tony no choice. He crossed to the platform where Moomaw waved him to Simon Frank's seat. "Tune up, Tony. Next one's *Sobre las Olas*."

"I'll mess it up," Tony predicted. But when Moomaw waved a wand he did his best. No one present was surprised. Substituting for the park's crack violinist was something Tony had done before.

Margie caught his eye and smiled. What would she think, Tony wondered, if she knew where he'd first learned to handle a fiddle?

Simon stayed away for two numbers. When he reappeared it was nearly midnight. Tony was crossing toward the exit when the stocky figure of Mark McCarron blocked his path.

"Wanta see you a minute." A stiffness in his employer's tone disquieted Tony. "Let's step outside."

Tony followed him into the lobby and from there to the hotel's small parlor. McCarron didn't sit down. He faced Tony with a half-doubtful smile. "Likely it's meant to be some kind of a joke, Tony. Just say it's not true and I'll tear it up." The hotel letterhead in McCarron's hand had words scratched on it. "Somebody gave it to the porter and had him pass it on to me. Take a look."

The message said:

> You got a strayman that done time for stealing horses. If you don't believe it, check with the warden at the Missouri state pen.

"Just say it's not so," McCarron repeated, "and I'm satisfied."

Blood crept up Tony's neck. As he hesitated McCarron waved his cigar impatiently. "Well, what about it?"

Thought of lying didn't occur to Tony. Here was a crisis he'd always dreaded, a corner into which he'd hoped never to be driven. His lip trembled as he met it head-on. "I was two years in prison, Mr. McCarron. But I never stole a horse or anything else."

A cigar dropped to the rug. The plump face of McCarron seemed to swell as though a deadly poison had stung him. "You mean you admit it? You're a jailbird?"

The term hurt Tony and his voice took an edge. "Call me that if you want. It won't make me guilty of what I didn't do."

McCarron stood staring. He was a man of

quick judgments and usually they were fair. Tony waited desperately for this one. Odor from a burning rug made McCarron stamp out a cigar. This one had been lighted. McCarron picked it up, crossed to an open window, threw it out. When he turned a stony condemnation was on his face.

"A court said you were. A jury said you stole horses. You served time."

"You don't believe me?"

"I'd like to." The flatness of the man's tone made a wall between them. "All I know for sure is you came straight from a prison cell to my payroll. And began setting up to Margie. That much I can put a stop to." He brought thirty dollars from his pocket. "Here's a month's pay in lieu of notice."

Tony gaped at him. He'd worked a whole year for McCarron. "You're firing me?"

"What do you expect me to do? Keep sending you out to rep me at roundups? Your case was tried once. In court. It's not my business to try it again. You've stuff at the bunkhouse. Where do you want it sent?"

A pleading came into Tony's voice. "Won't you sit down, please, and let me tell you just what happened?"

"You're a year too late." The wall was high and cold, now, like granite. "You should have told me when you first came to the ranch."

Tony wanted to say he'd planned telling them just as soon as he found Memphis Jack. The only man in the world who knew he was innocent. But it would sound lame and hopelessly unconvincing.

"Take my advice," McCarron said, "and get clear off this range. Or if you stay in the park make a clean breast to your next boss before you start eating at his table. I'll send your stuff into town."

The rancher walked to the door, then whirled about. "And look: stay away from Margie."

Tony gave him a tight smile. "That goes for the next dance? Happens my name's on her card."

"It goes for right now and for all time." It was McCarron's last word as he left the parlor. Its finality dashed Tony but he checked an impulse to follow and argue. Or even to make an issue of the dance.

He'd succeed only in embarrassing Margie. Her father would try to break it up and there'd be a scene on the floor. No sense in putting the girl on a spot like that. He had a feeling she'd take his side. But it would mean a quarrel with her father and that wouldn't be fair.

Tony went no further than the lobby. Young Billy Adams was standing there and Tony said to him: "Look, Billy. Something came up and I have to pull out. You mind handling the next one for me? It's with Margie McCarron."

A grin creased Billy's face. "Can a duck swim?" he assented.

"Thanks." Tony left the hotel and crossed State Avenue. He was turning the corner when a rider he knew stopped him.

"Somethin' you oughta know, Tony. Come in and I'll buy you one."

Tony was in no mood for it. But there was something ominous in his friend's tone. His guess was that Lew Wager had passed his spite tip to others than Mark McCarron. "Okay, Chuck; let's hear it." He followed Chuck Gleason to Slavick's bar.

Gleason took a whisky and Tony a short beer. "You know a guy named Tully? Long skinny guy that used to deal faro up at Saguache?"

"Know him by sight. What about him?"

"He was shootin' off his mouth in here," Gleason confided, " 'bout an hour ago. I heard him. So did Slavick and his customers. Later this jigger sashayed down to the Peso de Oro and made the same talk. He's doin' it there right now."

"What kind of talk?"

"Gun talk. He's likkered up and he's heeled on both hips. It's all about you, *amigo.* Claims he's gonna blow five-six holes right through your middle."

"Did he say why?"

"Claims you done him dirt. He didn't say what it was."

The beer tasted bitter and Tony pushed it away. "Thanks, Chuck. I'll keep my eyes open."

Gleason glanced at Tony's beltless waist. "Fat lota good it'll do you, all dolled up for a party and no gun on. Better take mine and let it chaperone you to bed."

Tony's impulse was to say no. It was only a block down Front to the Victoria. Then he remembered the Peso de Oro was in that block. He'd have to pass it to get home.

Gleason held out his cartridge belt with a forty-five in the holster. "Might as well take out insurance, *amigo*."

He might avoid an encounter, Tony thought, by circling the block. But why let himself be chased off a direct and natural path by a thug like Tully? His humiliation at the hands of McCarron was stinging deep. And one humiliation was enough for tonight.

"Thanks, Chuck." Tony buckled on the belt and gun.

"What'd you do to that buzzard?" Gleason inquired curiously.

"Nothing he won't get over. Was he alone when you saw him?"

"All by himself."

Tony recalled the man's parting with Lew Wager. They'd seemed to be in some disagreement and the nature of it wasn't hard to guess. They had a common motive of ill will against

Tony. Each would want to strike back. But Wager, slyer and more cautious, had chosen to get even merely by sending a spite note to Tony's boss. Which to Tully would seem far too tame a reprisal.

"All by himself," Chuck repeated, "down at the Oro bar. He was peelin' an eye on the front walk, last I saw of him. Somebody tipped him you're bunkin' at the Victoria. So he knows you'll pass right by on the way to bed."

Tony nodded toward a corner table. "I got something on my chest, Chuck." He went to the table, Chuck trailing after him.

"Spill it, partner," Chuck invited.

"There's a bare chance Tully might knock me over. I don't expect him to, but it could happen. Tonight in front of the Oro."

Chuck nodded. "He's ridin' a hot grudge, and he's just drunk enough to cut loose on sight."

"Look, Chuck. Case he gets me I want you to pass something on to Margie McCarron. I mean—tell her why her dad fired me."

Gleason gave a wide-eyed stare. "Fired you? When?"

Tony nodded. "Forget it if I get by Tully tonight. If I don't, I want Margie to know the whole story."

Gleason rolled a cigaret, his gray eyes narrow and full of understanding. "Shoot, *amigo*."

Tony began with what he'd told Helga Tarber, how at six he'd been bound out to an Indiana farmer from whom he'd run away at the age of twelve. "I worked and begged my way across three counties, Chuck. After I'd crossed into Illinois a coupla tramp horse traders named Tolliver picked me up. They had a camp wagon and a string o' crow-bait broomtails. You've seen outfits like that. They travel through the North in the summer and drift south in the winter—trade any horse they got for any other horse just so long as they get boot."

"Sure," Chuck put in. "Neither horse is any good. But after each trade they still got a horse and a little cash boot."

"Usually they had about thirty nags on hand," Tony said. "Which made plenty of camp chores for a twelve-year-old kid. I made fires and washed dishes. While they were off trading, I herded the string left at camp. We traveled down through Tennessee and Arkansas. And those Tollivers—brothers they were—treated me a heap better'n I'd ever been treated before. Podge Tolliver had a fiddle and he taught me to play it. Ferg Tolliver'd had schoolin' in his better days and he passed some of it on to me. We lived around campfires and in old deserted farmsteads—just like a family."

"For how long, partner?"

"For the best part of six years. Six kid years, Chuck. What a kid I was! I was eighteen when the blow-up came."

"You mean they went crooked?"

"I think they kept straight till about the last year, Chuck. The way they worked was like this: we'd camp at good free pasture and I'd stay with the stuff that was too skinny to trade. Podge and Ferg'd go off with maybe twenty of the best broncs and be gone a week at a time. They'd come back with twenty different horses, plus cash boot, and we'd move to another county. I thought they were trading horse for horse. But toward the end they were *selling* what they went out with—and *stealing* what they brought back."

Chuck whistled. "Whatta racket!"

"We were camped in the Missouri Ozarks when they brought in eighteen new horses. I was herdin' them to water when the posse came. They grabbed me and the Tollivers lit out. Bullets chased them, knocked them dead out of their saddles. Nobody believed me when I said I thought the nags had been fair-traded. All I could prove was I'd been livin' family-style with the Tollivers for six years. I had no money for a lawyer. The court gave me three years and I got out in two."

Something soft and gentle came into Chuck's eyes and spread over his blistered, sand-whipped face. He was eight years older than Tony. "That sure was a raw deal, fella. You hit west, then, and got a job with McCarron?"

"Tonight he found out about it," Tony finished bitterly, "and gave me the sack."

"He'll change his mind," Gleason predicted, "once he thinks it over. Mark don't usually throw a man down like that. He's apt to fly off the handle, though, if anybody mentions horse thieves. Remember last Fourth of July?"

Tony did, but hadn't thought of it till now. Ten months ago thieves had made off with some Wagon Wheel horses and in the chase Tommy McCarron, Mark's only son, had been killed by the fugitives.

Tony stood up, checked the loads in the borrowed gun. "Don't say anything about this, Chuck, if I get by Tully tonight."

As he started out Chuck Gleason followed him to the door. "I might as well amble along with you, fella."

"Rather you wouldn't, Chuck." The suggestion that he needed protection irritated Tony and he motioned his friend back.

He went out alone and turned east along the Front Street walk. Mercantile shops were dark, now, but saloons in the block were ablaze with lights. Idlers in front of the Brakeman's Lantern flattened themselves against the wall as Tony came abreast. One of them warned, "Look out for trouble, kid." And from another: "They's a guy with a gun down the street a bit. When you see him, see him first."

Tony went on past the Alva Adams store and just beyond lights from the Peso de Oro made a yellow swath across the walk.

The let-down, half a minute later, made him feel foolish. He came opposite the shoulder-high twin doors of the Oro and nothing happened. Glancing sidewise over them Tony saw men at the bar—but Tully wasn't among them.

He moved on, boots thumping the planks, and came to the corner of Hunt. Directly across it two tarp-covered wagons were parked for the night. They were still loaded with the assets of a bank, and under each wagon a driver lay asleep in his blankets. Tony turned left and a few steps took him to the Victoria Hotel's entrance.

A buzz of talk leaked from the lobby but the street itself was quiet. Quiet until Tony started up the porch steps of the hotel. Then a shot rang out. Its bullet splintered a porch post and a high-pitched voice came with it. "Say your prayers, cowboy!"

A second shot breathed on Tony before he could whip out his gun. The slug shattered a lobby window. Tully stood spread-legged a little way up the walk, holding a gun with both hands and blazing away. Liquor-inflamed hate had eaten all discretion and the man's only thought was to kill.

But liquor and hate had also spoiled his aim. His third shot came coincident with Tony's first and Tony didn't need to shoot again. He saw

Tully drop the gun and use both hands to clutch at his stomach. As the man jackknifed on the sidewalk a dozen men ran toward him, most of them from the hotel lobby.

A medley of yelling reached Tony. “He was layin’ for you, mister.” Another said: “I seen the whole play, fella. Nothin’ else you could do.”

Tully, when Tony got to him, was dead.

5

At nine Monday morning Coroner Celestino Romero arrived from Conejos and opened the first of two inquests at Town Hall in Alamosa. His six-man jury had already heard three witnesses when Tony's turn came.

"You heard the shot?" Romero had a salt-and-pepper goatee and a voice as soft as feathers.

"I heard it," Tony said.

"You saw Pancho Morales fall dead?"

"He was dead, time I got there."

"Did you see who fired the shot?"

"Not even his smoke. Sounded like it came from between two boxcars."

"Can you add to the testimony already given?"

"Not a thing," Tony said.

"Thank you, señor."

Other eye witnesses gave substantially the same answers. Undersheriff Milt Yeager was then called.

"Did the deceased have any known enemies?"

"None I can dig up," Yeager testified. "He worked off and on as a cook in a Front Street beanery. Seemed to get along all right with his boss and the customers."

"When killed, was he wearing a gun?"

"Nope. But I found this in his pocket. And it's

kinda got me buffaloed. Take a look, coroner." Yeager laid a paper on the table.

"This," Celestino Romero announced after an inspection, "is from the land office at Del Norte. It approves an application made by one Eusebio Sanchez to homestead a quarter section of land." The coroner's eyes narrowed as he added: "But this should be in the possession of Eusebio Sanchez since it is he who files on the land. Why does another man, Pancho Morales, have it in his pocket?"

"That's what I can't figure out," Yeager said. "The land filed on is up Poso Creek, twenty mile southwest o' here. Sunday I sent a man up there to look for Eusebio Sanchez. No sign of him. It's a bare quarter without even a footprint on it. And here in town I can't find anyone who ever heard of Eusebio Sanchez."

Tugging at his goatee the coroner puzzled over it. "He files an application for land which the land office approves, yet the approval is found on a dead man with the name of Morales! You will inquire further into this, Señor Yeager?"

"I sure will," Yeager promised.

The jury conferred briefly and arrived at a verdict: that Morales had met death at the hands of an unknown assassin.

Promptly the coroner called his second inquest of the morning. An inquiry into the killing of one Frank Tully, formerly of Saguache and Del Norte.

"I've dug up a dozen men," Yeager testified with a tolerant smile toward Tony Darrow, "who heard Tully brag he was gunning for Darrow and was gonna pump him fulla holes on sight. I dug up five others who saw the gunplay. They all saw Tully cut loose twice before Darrow even got his gun out. An open and shut self-defense, coroner."

Other witnesses confirmed this. One of them added: "That Tully was a bad one, coroner. I knew him up at Saguache. Get him mad and give him a coupla drinks and he'd as lief kill as look at you."

Tony began to hope he wouldn't even be questioned. Everyone present, including the editor of the *Weekly Independent* who stood by taking notes, seemed satisfied that he was blameless. Five of the jurymen made shuffling sounds as though anxious to have it over.

Then one juror, curious rather than hostile, asked that Tony be sworn as a witness.

The juror's first question: "How come the guy had it in for you, cowboy?"

Tony's eyes veered in an unspoken protest to the coroner. But Romero smiled and ruled softly: "It is the privilege of any juror to ask what he wishes. You will answer, señor."

"I had a little argument with him one time," Tony evaded, "and he got the worst of it."

"What kind of an argument?" the juror persisted. "Any gunplay in it?"

"Nothing to speak of. Nobody was hurt."

Tony had never been a good dissembler and his uneasy flush only sharpened the juror's insistence. "When was this?" "What was it all about?" "Let's have the straight of it, cowboy." Question followed question and each got Tony in a little deeper. The newspaperman's pencil flew faster as he scented a sensational background of motive.

Finally the coroner himself took up the questioning. "You say you disarmed him, señor, to prevent him from holding up wagons? How could you know he planned such a crime? And why did you not inform the law?"

"I had nothing to go on," Tony floundered, "only I saw 'em buyin' ammunition at Del Norte. They had grain sacks and masks in their saddlebags."

The coroner's eyebrow went up. "They? Tully and who else?"

"Tully and a man named Wager." Tony bit hard on his lip. His mention of Wager would make them try to pick up Wager for questioning. And Wager's answers were easy to foresee. He'd swear that he and Tully had been riding peacefully down the road when Tony had held them up from ambush, after which he'd ridden off with their horses. And how could anyone prove otherwise?

The only possible chance, Tony now realized

with dismay, was to tell the truth, the whole truth, here and now.

"When I was a kid . . ." he began. . . .

The *Independent* came out on Thursdays and the Friday stage to Jasper usually tossed off Mark McCarron's copy as it rumbled up Alamosa Creek past the Wagon Wheel gate. This week Margie herself was standing at the gate. "Big doin's in town, Margie," the driver yelled as he went by.

Unfolding the paper she saw Tony Darrow's name in a tall headline. He'd killed a man, the paper said, and for that the county owed him a vote of thanks. A coroner's jury had dismissed it as an act of self-defense. Then Margie read a few lines further and was shocked breathless.

Tony had been in prison! For horse stealing! It just couldn't be true. Yet there it was, the whole story in his own words. But as Margie read it to the end, a complete and unreserved sympathy swelled inside of her. Poor Tony! Where was he now? Off alone on the range, she supposed, looking for Wagon Wheel strays. But it was no time for him to be alone! He should be at home with his friends where they could all stand by him and let him know they believed, as she did, that every word of his testimony was true.

Quite suddenly Margie remembered something. The dance Tony had abruptly canceled at the

Perry House. Billy Adams had taken his place. Why? Something must have gone wrong about then. Margie recalled, too, the stern preoccupation of her father. He'd hustled her into a buckboard at two in the morning and driven her swiftly to the ranch. As a rule, after a party like that, they stayed all night in town. Nor had he offered any explanation.

Since then Mark McCarron had barely spoken to her. He'd seemed almost to avoid her. Now a terrible suspicion came to Margie. One that shamed her and then angered her and brought defiant sparks to her eyes. Her face took a militant set as she walked quickly to the house, skirts swishing.

A log ell of it was Mark McCarron's office. Margie found him there. Trouble rode his broad ruddy face as he sat idle at his desk, chewing a cold cigar. "Mail come?" he asked, then blinked at the newspaper in her hand.

As she laid it in front of him she could see that the tall headline gave him no reaction of surprise.

"You knew it before we left town!" she charged. "That's why Tony didn't dance with me. You told him not to!" She gave it as a shameful fact, not as a question.

McCarron put down the cigar. He answered her in a tone of dull but irrevocable finality. "I fired him. He won't be back."

"But read what it says!" Margie demanded. "He

explains everything. Every single thing. He was just a boy. He didn't know those horses were . . ."

"He says he didn't," her father cut in. "A court said he did. He gave me the same yarn Saturday night. All we know for sure is he served time for stealing horses." McCarron stood up. "He's through at the Wagon Wheel. I sent Clem in with his two nags and his bedroll."

Margie stood back from him, mortified, shocked to the edge of tears. "But we're his friends!" she protested desperately. "His people! This ranch is his home. If *we* don't stand by him, who will?"

"He can hit for another range." McCarron's stand was stone, without a crack of compromise in it. "I told him that at the hotel. He can hit for another range and start over."

A bleak thought came to Margie: perhaps he'd already gone! It was easy to foretell that other ranches in the park would shy at taking him on. "He did time for stealing horses," they'd say. "McCarron gave him the sack," they'd say. "If Mark can't trust him, why should we?"

"I think it's perfectly rotten, treating him like that!" Margie's five feet two inches of blazing bitterness stood tempestuously up to her father. "Turning him out like a rat just because some stupid jury made a mistake long ago! He couldn't any more steal a horse than I could, or you could, or Blaise could, or . . ."

Her use of Blaise Amory's name flashed an idea to her mind. To act on it, the girl whirled out and hurried down to the barn. Clem, the choreman, was cleaning up there. "Hitch up my buggy mare, Clem. I'm going to town."

"Yes'm." Clem thought nothing of it as he took down a set of single harness. Margie often went to town on a whim.

By the time he'd hitched up she'd been to the house and was back again. This time she had on a town dress, a hat, gloves and a veil. Also a small bag as though she might stay all night at a hotel.

As Clem handed her into the buggy Mark McCarron strode toward them. The rancher had a grim look. "Where are you going?" he demanded.

"To town." Her chin high, Margie touched her whip to the mare's flank and was off. She knew he wouldn't try to stop her. Since her mother's death, five years back, he'd discovered it was no use trying to control Margie when she took the bit between her teeth like this. A shade of gray chased the ruddiness from McCarron's face as he stood there, frustrated, and watched her drive out through the gate.

She followed downcreek to the main road and there turned north along the railroad line. There was as yet no passenger service below Alamosa but construction crews were pushing the track on toward Cumbres Pass. Margie kept the mare at a smart trot and knew she could make town by noon. The distance was only twelve miles.

Was Tony still there? After a few rebuffs in his hunt for another job he might give up and trail out of the park. Again Margie's whip touched the mare's flank and she shook the reins urgently. She must see Tony at once and show her own loyal colors.

She could do it by having lunch with him in Alamosa's most public spot, the Perry House dining room. Let the whole town, and all of San Luis Park, see that it had at least one citizen with loyalty enough, and decency enough, to stand by a friend in trouble.

And on her way home, Margie decided, she'd stop at Blaise Amory's place, the Jaybird. She'd make Blaise offer Tony a job.

At noon Margie wheeled down Fifth Street in Alamosa. And almost at once she saw Tony. He was on the sidewalk in front of Easterday's grocery store talking to a young woman. She was a tall, golden girl in what looked like a homespun dress, and Margie had never seen her before. But clearly Tony had; the two appeared to be on pleasantly familiar terms.

A brief dismay assailed Margie. At the moment Tony seemed to have all the sympathy he needed. And taking him to lunch, when he seemed already nicely equipped with company, might not be so simple after all. A spring wagon with a team of mules stood hitched at Easterday's tie rack. Margie drew up beside it. "Hello, Tony." If she was a bit disconcerted her blithe tone didn't show it. "Hitch for me, will you?"

She was out of the buggy before Tony could help her. He caught her hand just in time to hand her up on the high board walk. "Hi, Margie." He said it lightly, gayly. "You know Helga Tarber? She drove down from Del Norte to pick up some freight."

The tall golden girl smiled. "You're Margie McCarron? I've always wanted to know you."

How well, Margie wondered, did she know Tony Darrow? But she liked Helga at once. Helga was so completely genuine. "Thank you." Margie made her own smile no less warmly generous. "Is this the freight?" She glanced toward a crate on the spring wagon. "It looks like a sewing machine."

"It is," Helga said. "My father ordered it from Chicago."

Looking up at her gave Margie a faint tinge of envy. Not because of Tony Darrow but because she'd always secretly envied tall, capable girls like Helga Tarber.

"How long will you be in town?" Margie asked her.

"I'll go back tomorrow," Helga said. The distance was too far to drive in an afternoon.

“Then why don’t you have lunch with me right now?” Margie invited.

“That would be nice,” the tall girl agreed promptly, pleasure showing in her clear frank eyes.

Margie turned as though with a careless afterthought to Tony. “You too, Tony. Why don’t you stable our rigs for us and then meet us at the Perry House?”

All of Alamosa saw them in the dining room there—Margie and the strayman just discharged by her father. The tall blonde girl sharing a table with them served only to make the party more conspicuous. Everyone in town had read the *Independent*, had absorbed every rumor and fact. A new fact could be added now: Tony Darrow was still in good standing with Margie McCarron.

Which was exactly the way Margie wanted it. It publicly dramatized her disapproval of Mark McCarron’s action in Tony’s case and made it unnecessary for her to mention it at all.

The nearest she came to it was a mention of Blaise Amory. “By the way, Tony. Blaise Amory’s going to offer you a job at the Jaybird. You’ll take it, won’t you?”

Tony gave her a searching look. When he was sure she meant it, his face relaxed. “Why not? If he offers me a job I’ll take it all right. Six months out of the year, anyway.”

Margie knitted her brow over this. "Why not the year around, Tony?"

He grinned. "Didn't I tell you? I've filed me a homestead. Means I'll have to live on it part of the time, and build a shack there, in order to prove up."

"A homestead? Here in the park?"

Tony nodded. "On the lower Conejos about two miles above the old Pike stockade."

"Wonderful!" Margie applauded. "That isn't more than four miles from the Jaybird."

"About that. And less'n ten miles from the Wagon Wheel." Tony turned to Helga Tarber and explained, "Amory's Jaybird's on La Jara Creek just east of the track."

Helga had been attending with interest. "I've read about the Pike stockade," she said. "Zebulon Pike built it in 1807, just a little way up the Conejos from the Rio Grande."

"Not knowing," Margie put in, "that he was trespassing on Spanish territory."

"I've heard about Blaise Amory, too," Helga said. "Wasn't he the hero of the Conejos River massacre, six years ago?"

"The hero," Margie confirmed, "and the sole survivor. He doesn't like to talk about it, though; Blaise is really terribly modest and shy."

Tony's head jerked toward her to make sure she was serious. And quite clearly she was. In Tony's own observation the Jaybird man had been anything but modest or shy. Evidently he'd completely sold himself to Margie McCarron. To draw Margie out Tony asked innocently, "It was the Pablo Arragon outfit, wasn't it, that got wiped out?"

"That's right. A band of Utes had them surrounded and . . ."

"Begin at the start," Tony suggested. "I always did want to get the straight of that. How did Blaise happen to be working for the Arragons, anyway?"

"The Arragon hacienda," Margie explained, "was across the state line, in New Mexico. Seven years ago Blaise Amory came west from Virginia to chase wild horses. He says he was just an adventuring kid in those days, as wild as the horses he wanted to chase. Instead of catching them he lost his own and went limping around half-starved through the mountains where he was finally picked up by the local *rico*, Don Pablo Arragon. Don Pablo took him to the hacienda, nursed him back to health, and Blaise liked the life there so well he stayed almost a year."

Tony gave an understanding nod. "They'll give you the shirt off their back, those *gente* will."

"Wasn't it a sheep ranch?" Helga asked.

"A big one," Margie said. "In the summer of '74 Don Pablo started north with nine thousand head of sheep. He had a camp wagon and ten herders, including Blaise Amory. Blaise drove the wagon.

They grazed their way north across San Luis Park to Saguache, then over Pancho Pass and up the Arkansas to the gold camps around Oro City, Alma and Fairplay."

"A plenty long drive," Tony commented. "Grazin' along at four miles a day it'd take 'em about two months."

"Don Pablo sold his sheep at the mining camps for forty thousand dollars in gold coin." Margie told her story with relish. "Then they started back south. They crossed the Rio Grande about where we are now—but of course Alamosa didn't exist then. The park had no people at all west of the river, except around Conejos. East of the river the main settlements were Fort Garland and San Luis. Don Pablo's ten-man party, homeward bound, got as far as the Conejos River when the Utes attacked. Blaise says it came just at dawn when he was hitching up the wagon. War whoops and rifle bullets from every direction." Margie shuddered. "You can imagine how horrible it was!"

The rest was common knowledge throughout the park. Tony had heard the tale around roundup fires. How the Arragon party was surrounded and besieged in a cottonwood grove; three herders and the wagon mules killed in the first onslaught; the other seven men crouching back of windfall logs and trading bullets all day with the Indians. "The way I heard it," Tony said, "when night came Don Pablo asked for a volunteer to crawl through the Utes and make it afoot to Fort Garland."

"Blaise was the youngest and the boldest." Tony noted a glow of pride on Margie's face as she took up the tale. "So he volunteered. In the darkness he slipped through them by floating down the Conejos—he still has scars from the rock bruises he got in those rapids. By daylight he'd crossed the Rio Grande and was working his way up Trinchera Creek through brush and thorn and sage, on the old Beaubien Grant. In all he ran twenty-six miles and when he got to Fort Garland he was a mass of cuts and scratches. He fell exhausted just as a sentry challenged him there."

"I was in school at Del Norte," Helga Tarber remembered, "and the *Del Norte Prospector* had the news a few days later. A troop of cavalry rushed to the Arragon camp—too late."

It had all happened five years before Tony's arrival in the park. Yet he knew well enough what the cavalrymen had found there. Arragon and his herders dead and scalped. The wagon burned. The gold and the blanket rolls carried off by the raiders.

"This homestead I'm filing," Tony told them soberly, "is right at that spot. Nice piece of bottomland with plenty of wood along the river. I'll take out a ditch right some day."

Helga looked out and saw a covered wagon making dust up Front Street. "Another home-seeker," she observed. "They're coming in over Mosca Pass every day."

"Speaking of homesteaders," Tony said, "did you ever hear of one named Eusebio Sanchez? He filed a claim up Poso Creek lately."

Neither of the girls had ever heard the name.

"An approval from the land office," Tony told them, "was found on a dead man here in town. Pancho Morales."

Margie looked thoughtful. "Was he a cook?" she asked.

"He cooked in a beanery, off and on. You know him?"

"A Pancho Morales," Margie remembered, "applied at our ranch for a job as cook. Father didn't like his looks and turned him down. But he had a reference from some lawyer here in town. A lawyer named Saul Spengler."

Helga stood up reluctantly. "Thank you for inviting me to lunch, Margie. Right now I have to go out and buy supplies and do a dozen errands. It's been awfully nice. Goodbye, Tony."

As she left them Tony called after her, "Don't let the wolves get you, Helga."

Margie gave him a straight look. "And just what, please, would you mean by *that?*"

6

Lettering on a second-floor window over Easterday's grocery announced:

SAUL SPENGLER
ATTY & NOTARY PUBLIC

Tony, after leaving Margie at the Perry House, climbed the narrow, shabby steps to Spengler's office. He knew of Spengler as a down-and-outer, a lawyer in name only, an alcoholic rarely sober enough to appear in court. But the man *did* have a notary seal and occasionally earned fifty cents by notarizing a deed or contract.

The office door was open and Tony heard Spengler even before he saw him. The notary sat at his untidy desk, disheveled, unshaven and snoring. An empty whisky pint lay on the desk. Dust shrouded everything and cobwebs draped the ceiling. The man himself was fat and gross-featured. Fleshy smells came from the anteroom he used for living quarters. A threadbare coat, shiny with age and one which in better days he'd worn in courtrooms, hung on a chair. Saul Spengler was collarless, his stained shirt bulging outward over the fleshiness of his neck and torso.

Tony stood looking at him with a huge distaste. “Wake up,” he said, and shook the man.

Presently Spengler sat up, blinking blearily from bloodshot eyes. He fumbled for a notary seal and made ready to use it, under the impression that Tony had come to sign some paper.

“All I want to know,” Tony said, “is when was the last time you saw Pancho Morales.”

The man jerked a little. His moist eyes contracted and all at once he was cautious. He cleared his throat. “Pancho Morales? I don’t seem to recall the name. Why do you ask?”

“Somebody sniped a slug through him last Saturday night. Milt Yeager’s tryin’ to get a line on him. Turns out he applied for a ranch job one time, as a cook. He had a letter of recommendation from you, Spengler.”

“Did he? Well, perhaps he served me one time. Or perhaps he was a client. I can’t remember. Now if that’s all”—the notary made a feeble motion of dismissal—“I’m not feeling too well. So if you’ll please . . .”

“What about a fellow named Eusebio Sanchez?” Tony cut in. “Ever hear of him?”

The man’s caginess grew. He made a pretense of straightening papers on the desk. “Sanchez? The name isn’t familiar. Why ask me about him?”

“A paper belonging to Sanchez was in Morales’ pocket. A land office paper.”

“As a mere notary,” Saul Spengler said quickly, “I’m not eligible to acknowledge land office papers." Which was quite true. Only a land office official, like Guy Halderman, or the clerk of a county court, was allowed to acknowledge either the original or final papers on a homestead filing.

Yet an item in the desk litter in front of Spengler caught and held Tony's eye. It was the name Eusebio Sanchez. It was addressed on an empty envelope postmarked Del Norte and which had been received at the Alamosa post office. Printing at the envelope's upper left corner proved it had been sent out by the U. S. Land Office at Del Norte. The address was: Eusebio Sanchez, General Delivery, Alamosa, Colorado; and the postmark was a month old.

"You say you don't know him?" Tony pointed at the envelope.

A hint of fright mottled the caution on Spengler's face. He licked his thick, fleshy lips and stirred uneasily. "Lots of people come in here for advice," he offered, "or to get papers notarized. One of them may have dropped an old envelope." He adjusted glasses to the bridge of his strawberry nose and looked at this one. "I can't remember seeing it before."

Tony went down to the street. The Sanchez envelope, after a moment's thought, didn't seem so important. Sanchez might have brought his filing approval to this cheap lawyer to ask what, if anything, needed to be done next. The envelope might drop unnoticed on the desk. How the enclosure had later come into the possession of Pancho Morales would be a matter strictly between Sanchez and Morales.

Tony stepped into the Perry House to look for Margie but she was gone. He was about to go out again when he saw Saul Spengler. The shabby attorney, encased now in his shiny black coat, was moving at an impatient pace down the State Avenue walk. *He's heading for Slavick's,* Tony thought, *for another pint.*

But Spengler didn't turn in at Slavick's. He rounded the corner and sped east along Front. Maybe the man preferred the Peso de Oro, Tony thought. He himself strolled that way, since his next stop would be his own room at the Victoria. Idly he watched the short, bulky figure of Spengler bowl along ahead of him. And again the man passed a saloon without turning in.

At the corner of Hunt, Spengler went into the Victoria Hotel. Tony himself arrived in the lobby just in time to see the notary scurry upstairs. Tony was halfway up the steps when he heard a knocking in the hall above. As his eyes came level with the matting there, he saw Saul Spengler at the door of number seven.

"Let me in, Blaise." The notary's voice had an edge of apprehension. "Something you ought to know."

Number seven's door opened and Tony glimpsed Blaise Amory. The Jaybird owner wore a lounging robe. He seemed annoyed as he admitted Spengler and closed the door.

Tony went on up and into his own room. He sat on the bed, puzzlement creasing his forehead. Why would Spengler race straight to Blaise Amory?

Then, startled, Tony remembered something. Saturday evening another man had knocked at that same door. And had *not* been admitted. After which he'd gone to the marshal's office to camp on the steps. While there he'd been shot dead. With a paper in his pocket belonging to Eusebio Sanchez! Sanchez whom nobody could now find!

And yet the same Sanchez who'd been a recent client of Saul Spengler. The same Spengler who, when questioned on the point by Tony, had come hotfooting to Blaise Amory!

A circle! A complete circuit running from Amory to Morales to Sanchez to a no-good lawyer and then back to Amory! What did it mean? Hidden within that circuit was there a motive for the murder of Morales?

Tony waited till he heard Spengler emerge from number seven. He went out then and followed the man down to the street. Where would the notary go next?

The question was quickly answered when Spengler turned into the Peso de Oro. Tony got there in time to see him spin a fifty-cent coin on the bar. "Whisky," was the husky, eager demand.

Spengler's hand shook as he raised it to his lips.

Tony took a stand beside him. "Blaise a client of yours?" he asked genially.

Spengler's blood-mottled eyes veered toward him and his mouth hung open. Then a cagey wait as the man seemed to fish for some plausible answer. Possibly they'd seen Tony's head appear above the stair well just as Amory opened the door.

"What makes you think he'd be?" the notary hedged.

"You just paid him a call. What for?"

Another wait before Spengler made response. When he did it came with a sly and calculated assurance. "I passed him a tip, if it's any of your business. Once he tried to buy the corner of Fourth and Hunt but it wasn't for sale. Little while ago I found out it's on the market so I told Blaise about it." The man gave an uneasy grin. "Blaise appreciated it, too, because he gave me a dollar." To prove it, Spengler produced a second fifty cent coin and rattled it down the bar. "More whisky," he demanded.

His smirk followed as Tony left the saloon.

Ten minutes later Tony was in Milt Yeager's office reporting the Spengler incident. The Blaise Amory angle of it didn't impress Yeager. "Look, Darrow, you can leave Blaise out of it. He's a top citizen. He wouldn't have any truck with a jackleg like Spengler. Spengler tries to mooch off him, sure. It'd be like him to run to Blaise with a tip like that, hoping for the price of a drink. Forget Amory. But this Sanchez envelope is something else."

"You mean you've located Sanchez?"

"Nope. But I checked with Receiver Halderman at the Del Norte land office. Sanchez' homestead application is on file there. He signed it in front of the county court clerk at Conejos, then mailed it to the land office; the land office mailed him the usual preliminary approval. The Conejos court clerk says he remembers Sanchez as a pint-size Mexican with droopy black mustaches. The trail ends right there. Except for this envelope you saw on Spengler's desk. Something funny about it, Darrow. Something dagged funny!"

Tony left the undersheriff wagging his head and went to Wilkins' livery barn. Margie McCarron's rig was gone so he knew she'd left for the ranch. Helga Tarber's mules were still there.

A few stalls deeper Tony took a look at his own animals. These were a calico saddler and a plump bay pack mare. McCarron had sent them into town, the same messenger collecting the Wagon Wheel mount on which Tony had last cruised for strays.

He gave the calico a slap on the flank. "You'll eat me broke," he grinned, "if I don't get you on grass pretty soon." According to Margie, Blaise Amory would offer him a job. And he'd promised to accept. His guess was that she'd come to town looking for Amory, intending to ask him point-blank to put Tony on the Jaybird payroll.

Perching on a saddle rack Tony rolled a cigaret. Two hours ago he'd been eager to get on at the Jaybird. His closest friend worked there. Chuck Gleason. There was no one on the range he'd rather ride with than Chuck.

But now he had doubts about Amory himself. Why was Amory tied up with people like Morales and Spengler? If he wasn't on the level, Tony had no stomach for a job with him. A man is judged by the company he keeps and it can lead him into grief. No one knew that better than Tony Darrow. Keeping company with the Tolliver brothers had led him to prison. He hadn't *known* they were bad company but . . .

He'd better evade Amory till he could think it over. That would mean getting out of town for a day or two. Where could he go? The Wagon Wheel bunkhouse, now closed to him, had been his only home in the park.

Sight of his bedroll gave him an idea. McCarron had sent the bedroll in with the two horses. Tony found the barman and paid his bill. "I'm leaving you for a while, Dave."

It was still only midafternoon when he rode out of Alamosa, leading a laden pack mare. His mood was up again and he was whistling. The range to every horizon looked good to him. Snowy walls on either side with a black and green floor between. The black of sage and the green of grass, and cottonwoods beginning to make leaf along the streams. Far to his left, beyond the Rio Grande, Tony saw antelope race down the wind, heads bobbing above the sage. Over there it was all Costilla County and the great Sangre de Cristo private grant. Over here it was open land, free range, nearly all of it as yet unclaimed and waiting for wagon-borne settlers.

Tony cocked his high wide hat aslant and spurred to a trot, the well-fed mare keeping easily apace. He rode proudly, reins held chin-high, with a smile on his lips and a song in his heart. A poison was gone from his life—the poison of a secret too long kept. Now that it was over he could even thank Lew Wager for forcing it into the open. What difference did it make that Mark McCarron had fired him? Margie was still on his side and so were Helga Tarber and Chuck Gleason. He'd just filed land of his own, hadn't he? It was springtime and he had a horse between his knees and blankets to sleep on. What more could a man want?

A bunch of Jaybird heifers grazed by the trail. Further on Tony sighted a lone Wagon Wheel bull, bawling petulantly for his lost herd.

Presently Tony reined left across the narrow-gauge track and a few miles further on he forded

La Jara Creek. On its far bank he drew up at the Jaybird barn. A neat rock ranch house had the shutters drawn. But a ringing of hammer on anvil came from a near-by shed.

Tony looked in there and saw Chuck Gleason shaping a horseshoe. The cowboy wore a leather apron to keep sparks from his shirt and chaps. Sight of Tony brought a grin to his sandpaper face. "Hi, *amigo.* You're just a half hour too late."

"Too late for what?"

"To see Margie McCarron. She just driv by here on her way home to the Wagon Wheel."

"What did she want, Chuck?"

"She wanted to see the boss. I told her he's in town. So she left a message for him with the Chinaboy cook."

Tony built himself a cigaret. "Look, Chuck. I got a tip I'm goin' to be offered a bunk here at the Jaybird. What kind of an outfit is it?"

The question brought a curious stare from Gleason. "You mean: is it on the level? Sure it is. I'm ridin' for it myself, ain't I?"

"The crew's okay," Tony agreed. "I know 'em all. But what about Amory himself? He wouldn't be mixed up in something shady, would he?"

Gleason smiled tolerantly. "See here, Tony. If anybody's been feedin' you dirt on Blaise Amory, forget it. He puts on the dog, sure. But he runs a square outfit and you can bet your shirt on it."

"What about fake filings on government land?" Tony persisted. "It's been done, I hear. Big ranches get bigger that way. The rancher gets a lot o' peons and drifters to file claims adjoining him and then sign 'em over to him when they prove up."

Chuck scoffed at the idea. "Sure it's been done. But not by Blaise Amory. The only deeded land on the Jaybird is a school section he bought from the state at public auction. All the adjoining land is still public domain and nobody's ever filed on it. Blaise speculates in town lots, once in a while, and he'll pick up a land bargain anywhere in the park if it's offered to him cheap enough. It's all on record at the courthouse."

"Okay, Chuck. I'll take your word for it." Tony thumped away his cigaret. "Time I'm shoving along now."

"Shovin' where, *amigo*?"

"I've filed me a quarter section," Tony told him, "over on the Conejos. Guess I'll bed down there tonight—just to see if it makes me feel at home."

He rode on southeasterly, leading the mare. Between creeks the valley was treeless; for miles in all directions Tony could see no house or fence other than Amory's. The McCarron place, off to the west and beyond the track, was marked only by the faint, distant line of the Alamosa Creek cottonwoods. Beyond it the land banked steeply to the piny San Juans. Chuck no doubt was right, Tony brooded. Amory stood high around here. High in the councils of the San Luis Park Live Stock Association and ace high with Mark McCarron.

The question was—how high did he stand with Margie?

Tony topped a slight swell and could see the Conejos River tree line. At a bend of it he had months ago picked his own fertile quarter section. An *alamosa* there—a grove of mature cottonwoods—meant firewood and shelter. Its wide, rich bottomland had a little sage on it, but mostly it was sod—bunch grass and grama.

Nor was it strange he'd picked the same spot chosen as a campsite, six years ago, by the ill-fated party of Pablo Arragon. For Arragon, passing this way, would also select the best shelter for his men and the best grass for his mules. Tony had even found the exact spot of the massacre—the improvised fort where the Mexicans had made their last stand. A small square with windfall logs on two sides, a hastily thrown up dike of dirt on the third, a camp wagon on the fourth. Charred bits of the wagon were still there.

Sounds of an axeman chopping in the *alamosa* made Tony slow to a walk. His first thought was that some other homeseeker was choosing that spot for a filing. Or maybe it was only a casual camper stopping for the night.

The chopping broke off when Tony approached closer to the grove. He supposed that the chopper had seen him coming and was now waiting for him to arrive. But when Tony rode into the cottonwoods he saw no one at all. Nor heard anything except the murmuring riffles of the Conejos. No man or beast or camp. Yet a big windfall log had three separate axe bites, each fresh and bright. The axe itself wasn't in sight.

Then a sixth sense warned Tony he was being watched—that eyes were peering from behind a tree. If the eyes were hostile there was nothing he could do about it now. The man would have him covered. So Tony called out genially, "Hello there; anybody home?"

The friendliness of his voice and face may have impressed the watcher. For when he stepped suddenly into view the rifle in his hands wasn't aimed at Tony. The muzzle slanted downward. Tony grinned and held up both hands, palms forward. "Howdy. You've sure been choppin' hell outa that log. If it's any of my business, what's goin' on around here?"

The rifleman was young, tall and the color of rusty iron. His cheekbones were high and broad, his hair black and braided. Once Tony had glimpsed the great Ouray himself, chief of the Southern Utes. This young Indian had the same proud bearing, the same intelligent, coal-black eyes.

"You Jaybird rider?" The Ute gestured in the general direction of La Jara Creek.

Tony smiled and shook his head. "I don't ride for anybody just now. Filed me a claim on this bend of the river and thought I'd pay it a visit. Whatsa matter? You got some grudge against Blaise Amory?"

"Him your friend?" the Ute questioned warily.

"Nope." Tony sensed that the Indian was hostile to Amory. "Matter of fact, I don't know as I'd trust that fella very far. Why?"

"His tongue has a fork." The Ute said it with a biting emphasis, his eyes shifting to three axe-chopped bites in a log. "I, Unahwa, have proof." His thumb pointed at his own breast.

"That so?" Tony dismounted. To win the Indian's confidence he took off his gunbelt and hung it on the saddle horn. Then he walked to the log and sat on it, thus putting his saddle rifle well beyond his reach. "What you got against that guy Amory?"

Unahwa leaned his rifle against a tree. He held his right arm at full length upward. "His lie is this high," he stated. Then he reached both arms outward to full spread, adding: "And this wide. He has evil in his heart and a fork in his tongue."

The calm eloquence of it helped to convince Tony. "You said something about proof," he prodded. "What kinda proof?"

Unahwa took what he considered proof from

his jacket pocket and advanced to Tony. Face to face, he opened his palm and exposed three mushroomed bullets. At once Tony knew they were very old bullets fired long ago; and that they'd come from the three axe bites in a windfall log. The Ute had chopped around three old bullet holes till he'd probed out the lead.

"White man's bullets," Unahwa said. He stood there in erect dignity, a tall, iron-colored young man with a hawk's feather in his black felt hat, exposing the evidence to Tony Darrow. Then he turned abruptly to his rifle and picked it up. From back of the same tree he took an axe. Axe under one arm and rifle under the other, he marched off and disappeared among the upriver trees.

7

Tony didn't follow. He sat there through three cigarets, mulling it over. "White man's bullets!" Yes, definitely those bullets had *not* been fired by an Indian. *Because they weren't rifle bullets.* "They're slugs from a forty-five six-gun!" Tony said aloud, and the impact of it jolted him.

For this same log had made a breastwork for Pablo Arragon and his men, six years ago. Bullets fired into its outward side must have come from the besieging raiders. Raiders who, after the massacre, had scalped their victims in the manner of warring Utes.

Yet never had Tony heard of a revolver-shooting Indian. Indians were riflemen. They'd never been anything else since the first time long guns had been put on sale at trading posts. Long guns had done for Custer's command, four years ago in Montana. Mounted or afoot, Indians fought with rifles. Never with pistols.

And yet Blaise Amory, stone-bruised and thorn-scratched, had arrived breathless at Fort Garland to report an attack by Indians!

The evidence of Unahwa, Tony admitted, wasn't conclusive. It was possible that pistol bullets had been fired into the log at a later date; perhaps by campers in a mood for target shooting. Possible but not probable. A target was usually something like an empty can or an ace of spades. And target bullet holes were always in a cluster—three of them wouldn't be spaced ten inches apart along a four-foot log.

Tony unpacked his mare, hobbled her and turned her to graze. He offsaddled his calico pony and made camp. All the while his mind turned the bullet clews over and over. Indians? Pistol-packing Indians? Who ever heard of a holster-gun Ute?

As he made a fire and supper, Tony summoned back everything people had told him about the Arragon massacre. Nine men had been killed and scalped; forty thousand in gold had been stolen and the wagon burned—a typical Indian raid, people said. There'd been a demand for reprisals against the Utes. But from his village beyond the San Juans the great chief Ouray had denied that any of his own tribe had participated.

Yet San Luis Park at the time had been a Southern Ute hunting ground. Public opinion, based mainly on the testimony of Blaise Amory, had pronounced the Utes guilty, demanding that the entire tribe be hustled off to some barren reservation in Utah.

Now came an intelligent young Ute to gouge white man's bullets from a log.

To the left of the log lay another exhibit of the massacre. The charred wheel of Arragon's wagon. Looking at it now, Tony saw that two spokes and a felloe had been completely burned away. There it lay, a grim relic of the tragedy six years ago. A wagon wheel with a gap in it! A gap in the tale of a massacre! Who now was filling it in truthfully? Blaise Amory? Or Unahwa the Ute?

Unahwa, zealous to acquit his people of a crime, might himself have planted those slugs in the log.

Either Unahwa or Amory, Tony concluded, was a liar. And if Amory was a liar he was also much worse—a treacherous murderer who'd conspired with white outlaws to destroy the Arragon party for a split in the gold.

Night came and Tony sat with his back against an *alamo*, his boots stretched toward a fire. Amory the fancy horseman! Amory of the Jaybird ranch, gallant cavalier and cock-of-the-walk, so plausibly popular that he was even vouched for by square-shooting cow hands like Chuck Gleason.

Where, after the Arragon massacre, had Blaise Amory spent the succeeding three years? Mainly in Santa Fe, Tony had heard. And in '77 he'd reappeared in this Colorado park with funds sufficient to buy a school section, improve it with buildings and ditches, stock the neighboring range and hire a crew at top pay. Later he'd picked up a few real estate bargains here and there in the park. Not with money earned on his ranch. There hadn't been time for that. It made more sense to conclude he'd started with a share of Arragon's gold.

If so, what about the gang who'd conspired with him in the raid? What had they done with their share? Had they sloughed it off at gaming tables? Were they now hovering on the fringe of Blaise Amory's life? Had one of them, perhaps, been a Mexican named Pancho Morales?

And was Eusebio Sanchez merely an alias for Pancho Morales? If so no wonder Milt Yeager couldn't turn up Sanchez in the flesh.

And where did that old soak of a notary fit in?

Tony put out the fire and rolled in his blankets, soft night sounds all about him, the music of the river sweet in his ears. He fell asleep to dream not of a wagon wheel with a gap in it but of a home he'd build here. A pleasant little house on the river bank, in the shade of this *alamosa* and with an alfalfa smell coming through the window. A shadow, then, fell across the dream for the little house seemed to be empty. Locked and empty. Its owner was riding far away through hills and valleys, saddle-weary, inquiring everywhere for a man named Memphis Jack. For until he found Memphis Jack a curse would lie on him and he could never rest. He could never live in the pleasant little house or bring a woman there to share it with him.

The champing of his horse awakened Tony Darrow and his eyes opened to daylight. Magpies were chattering along the Conejos.

He bathed in the river and hung a glass on a tree to shave by. Soon he had bacon on a fire.

He hadn't yet made up his mind about Blaise Amory's job.

The bacon was good and the coffee still better. Tony was rerolling his pack when he saw a horseman coming. The horse was a golden-maned sorrel and came at a lope from the direction of La Jara Creek. The rider had a tall tan hat and wore gauntlets. The rising sun glinted on the silver trimmings of his saddle.

Blaise Amory! Tony picked up his gunbelt and buckled it on.

The man drew up in the grove with a hearty salute. "Hi, Darrow! Am I too late for breakfast?" He sat astride his show horse, the big stallion, looking solid and handsome and plausible.

"Gleason said I'd find you here," Amory went on without waiting for an answer. "Came early so I wouldn't miss you. Just want to say you've got a job at the Jaybird, Darrow. You can trail over there right now, if you like, and move in."

And Tony still wasn't sure. Was this man straight or crooked? Licking a cigaret, Tony gazed intently up into the mounted man's eyes. By now Amory had noticed the axe bites in the log. A faint flicker of uneasiness on his face gave

Tony the boldness to ask: "You had a gunfight here one time, didn't you? Gang of Utes raided you. Right here, wasn't it?"

The heartiness deserted Amory's voice and manner. His answer came with a slow, cautious tension. "Yes, about here, I think. Why bring it up now?"

"I didn't bring it up," Tony said. "A Ute Indian brought it up. He claims it wasn't Indians made that raid on Arragon's camp."

Amory stared hard at Tony, then at the axe bites in the log. His glance veered briefly to the charred remains of a wagon wheel. He moistened his lips. "Just what do you mean?"

The fear in his eyes wasn't proof; yet, weighed with everything else, it brought conviction to Tony. His decision was abrupt and irrevocable. "About that job, Amory. I think I'll skip it and prove up on my homestead."

Amory's cautious stare kept probing him. "Not sore at anything, are you?"

"No," Tony answered shortly. Lacking proof he would have preferred to let it go at that.

But the Jaybird man wouldn't drop it. "You've been looking for a job all week, ever since McCarron fired you. Three other outfits turned you down. Now you're turning *me* down. Mind saying why?"

Tony was still reluctant. Why make a charge he couldn't prove? On the other hand, suppose he let Amory ride away wondering what he knew? Wondering what the Indian had told Tony?

Pancho Morales, after knocking at Amory's door with some complaint, had been sniped from the dark. If that killing had been ordered by Blaise Amory, why wouldn't the same order go out again? It could happen today, tomorrow, from any dry gulch on the range, even on the streets of Alamosa. *So if I don't speak out now, I may never get a chance.*

"Mind saying why?" Amory repeated.

"Not if you're dead set on knowing. You read the *Independent*, I guess. You know I did two years in prison one time."

Amory nodded. "What's that got to do with passing up a job at the Jaybird?"

"When the judge sentenced me he made a little speech. He said a man's judged by the company he keeps. I'd kept company with some horse thieves named Tolliver. So in prison I had a long time to think it over. I decided the best way to keep outa trouble is to keep outa bad company. I promised myself I'd stick to good company, once I got out. And I have, so far."

Amory, astride the golden-maned stallion, gave a frozen smile. "Not trying to insult me, are you? You wouldn't say the Jaybird's bad company?"

"Not the crew," Tony said.

Then a shifting of Amory's stirrups warned him. The man's knees had moved slightly and his hand took a tighter grip on the reins. Tony remembered a week ago today on State Avenue. How Blaise Amory could control this show horse at will, could make him kneel, or prance, or rear . . .

The leap came right at him as though the horse were jumping a fence, and Tony himself was the fence. Thirteen hundred pounds of horse flesh plus the weight of a man—forehooves driving doomfully on a level with Tony's eyes. Only the split second of warning enabled Tony to fling himself aside.

The right forehoof missed him by inches as the stallion went plunging by. And Tony, reaching out, caught a grip on Amory's ankle. The jerk, as the horse plunged on, snatched rider from saddle. Amory hit the ground in a sprawl and Tony stood over him, boiling mad now. Amory had struck to kill, without warning, by riding him down.

He let Amory get to his feet. The man backed off a step, his face livid, his eyes on Tony's gun. "Don't worry about it," Tony said. He unbuckled the gunbelt and tossed it aside. "I wasn't dead sure about you," he said, "till you tried to ride me down."

He side-stepped as Amory came in swinging. The knuckles grazed Tony's cheek as his own cracked into Amory's chin. His other hand came up with a staggering hook. The Jaybird man swung again and Tony, ducking, belted him across the mouth with the back of his hand. He followed this with jabs to the stomach till the man bent double.

"Quit it," Amory begged. He went to his knees with his hands flat on the ground. "Quit it! I've had enough."

The easy surrender surprised Tony and gave him a new contempt for the man. "Okay. Climb your horse and ride."

The stallion had come to a stop with dangling reins. Its saddle had no scabbard. Amory got up and staggered a few steps that way. Suddenly he whirled and threw an egg-size stone at Tony's head. He'd picked it up when his hands had been flat on the ground and now it struck Tony above the eye. Blood spouted there as surprise and pain shocked Tony. And Blaise Amory plunged at him in a flying tackle.

The man's surrender had been faked and now his head rammed Tony's stomach. Tony went to his back, the wind out of him, and a spurred boot kicked him in the face. "You're a fool!" Amory said savagely, and kicked him again and again. Tony lay on his back, groggy and breathless, blood from the stone wound blinding him.

But at the next kick he grabbed an ankle and his desperate yank upset the man. Tony rolled away from him and scrambled to his feet. Amory was up too and racing for the gunbelt Tony had tossed aside. Tony threw himself forward to make the race with him, got there a stride too late as Amory jerked the forty-five from its holster. He blazed a bullet point-blank as Tony closed in.

The very closeness of the clinch made the bullet miss. There was no time for another one. Tony's punch swiveled Amory's head around. He caught the gun arm and twisted. Amory howled and dropped the gun as Tony's free hand clipped upward to the chin. The knees of Blaise Amory buckled. He went down and didn't get up. Tony stood over him, panting for breath.

He took out a handkerchief and swabbed blood from the cut on his forehead. But the stone had cut deep and the blood kept spouting there. He saw that Amory was out cold and not likely to revive very soon. So Tony brought court plaster from his pack and pasted it over the cut.

He looked at the sorrel stallion and decided not to let Amory get astride again. The man was full of tricks. He might try to ride Tony down again. To insure against it Tony hoisted him in reverse to the saddle so that he faced the horse's tail. Amory, still out, slumped like a bean sack there. Tony used pigging strings to tie his feet under the mount's belly; he tied the man's hands to the saddle horn back of him. Amory would now be unable to control the horse.

His tall fancy hat lay nearby. Tony filled it with

cold water from the river. This he dashed into Amory's face.

It took two dips to revive him. Tony put out his campfire as Amory sat upright in the saddle, groaning. "Don't fret too much," Tony said to him. "An hour from now you'll be at home in bed."

He saddled his calico pony and packed the mare. With a short lead rope on the stallion and a longer one on the mare, he rode out of the grove and took a beeline for the Jaybird ranch.

Twisting in the saddle he looked back. He couldn't see Amory's face. But he could hear curses choke from the man's throat.

"Only two kinds of people I'd do this to," Tony assured him. "One's a double-crossing dry-gulcher and the other's a dry-gulching double-crosser. You're both kinds, Amory."

Presently he rode into the Jaybird ranch yard, stopped at the stone house there. From it came a gaping Chinese houseboy. From a bunkshack rushed five gringo cowboys with Chuck Gleason among them.

"What the hell?" Foreman Ed Murdy demanded. Tony knew him, liked him, fully trusted him. He'd shared a roundup fire with the entire Jaybird crew.

He dropped the stallion's lead rope and thumbed toward the livid Amory. "We had a fight, Ed. Better put him to bed." To the others he gave a comradely wave. "So long, fellas. See you in town sometime."

Leading only the pack mare he rode out of the yard and took the Alamosa trail.

8

Tony crossed the railroad track and had hit the main road when Chuck Gleason caught up with him. "Let's have the straight of it, *amigo*. How'd you come to beat him up?"

Tony smiled mirthlessly. "Didn't your boss tell you?"

"He gave us a song and dance but I can't swallow it. Never knew you to act that way, Tony."

"How does he say I acted?"

"He claims he rode up peaceful and offered you a job. You turned him down. He asked if you were sore about anything and you began throwing punches. He had to fight you off. But he was bare-handed and pretty soon you whanged him cuckoo with your gun. Next he knew he was ridin' backward on his bronc."

"If he was bare-handed how did I get this?" Tony tapped the patched cut over his eye.

Chuck leaned from his saddle for a look. "He wears a ring with a stone in it. Claims he got in one or two pokes before you conked him."

"Here's what happened, Chuck." In the next three miles Tony gave him the full story, including Pancho Morales, Notary Spengler and a Ute named Unahwa. "But I didn't really have very much on him, Chuck, till he tried to kill me with his horse."

Gleason hooked a knee around his saddle horn and rolled a cigaret. "Most folks won't go for it, Tony," he concluded. "I will, but most folks won't. You've nothin' to show for it. Not even the three slugs this Ute buck dug out of a log."

Tony admitted it. Unahwa had walked off with his evidence. And even if he reappeared three old bullets in his hand would not, out of setting, prove or even suggest anything at all.

"Know what I think, Tony? I think you're on the short end of it until you dig up some deadwood on that guy. He's been the fair-haired boy around here for a long time. Take the McCarrons, for instance. You'd sound funny tellin' 'em that Unahwa skit."

"I'd sound even funnier," Tony agreed wryly, "tellin' 'em I got a hunch Amory's sitting in on some kind of a landgrabbing game with Saul Spengler."

"A land grab? How do you figger it?"

"I haven't figured. I'm on a limb," Tony grimaced, "and Amory can saw it off any time he wants."

"You'll have a heck of a time gettin' a cow job," Chuck predicted. "Every cowman in the park'll side with Amory."

Tony smiled dryly. "Maybe I can get a job on the railroad gang, laying track."

"Maybe I can too," Chuck said. They were at the edge of Alamosa and he stopped his pony. "So long, Tony."

"Where you going now, Chuck?"

"Back to the Jaybird and draw my time. If Amory's a two-timer I don't wanta work for him either." Chuck Gleason wheeled his horse and loped back toward the ranch.

His friend's loyalty worked like a tonic on Tony. By the time he turned in at Wilkins' barn he was whistling. "If Chuck Gleason shows up, tell him I'm at the Victoria."

The town ditch was running full down the far side of Fifth Street, making puddles wherever it spilled over. Planks made bridges across it at the tie racks. Teams lined these racks and the walk beyond was full of shoppers, mostly women, for on that side of Fifth there were no saloons. A man took a side of beef out of his wagon and toted it into Theo Emperius' butcher shop. Next to this a contractor's window had a sign announcing: Track Layers Wanted.

The end of track was now climbing Cumbres Pass and good pay could be had at the camps there. Tony was in half a mood to cross and sign up for a construction job. Then he saw a horseman dismount over there and go into a harness shop. He was Mark McCarron.

Sight of the man brought a stubbornness to Tony and his mind vetoed the construction job.

He belonged to a world of saddles, not of picks and crowbars. That was his element and neither Amory nor McCarron could run him out of it.

He'd have to get on some kind of a payroll, though, to make money enough to build a cabin on that homestead.

An open carriage drawn by plumed horses turned the corner of Hunt and swung west along Fifth. Its coachman was an ancient Negro wearing a plum-colored coat and a plug hat. In the carriage were six women, each with a painted face and each launching her smiles at the masculine citizenry of the town. It was a daily parade in Alamosa. Decent women on the sidewalks gave frozen stares. For this was China Pete, the town's notorious Mongolian madam, and five of her soiled doves. Daily she flaunted them before the eyes of men, west along Fifth and back east along Front, for which purpose she maintained the finest carriage in town.

Tony turned the other way and was accosted by a trail-weary immigrant who stood beside his covered wagon. A woman with an infant in arms was on the wagon seat while a teen-age boy, pony-mounted, rode herd on a pair of Jersey cows. The older man hailed Tony.

" 'Scuse me, mister. Can you tell us where the land office is?"

"At Del Norte," Tony said. "Thirty miles upriver."

"Alder Crik's up that way, ain't it? I got a brother-in-law filed a claim there and we figger to join him."

Tony smiled, nodding. "Yeh, it's right at this end of Wagon Wheel Gap. That's the Narrows of the Rio Grande where she comes into the park."

The immigrant filled a corncob pipe. "We been wagon-wheelin' quite a piece, mister. All the way from Illinoy."

"You came in over Mosca Pass?"

"Yeh, my brother-in-law writ me to come that way. He said the water comes in through Wagon Wheel and the wagon wheels come in over Mosca." Grinning at his joke the man climbed back on his outfit.

Here, Tony thought as he moved on, was exactly the type of sincere homeseeker for which the Homestead Act existed. This family's entire life would soon be bounded by a quarter section of land. And a legion of others like them would soon be trailing west.

At the Victoria the clerk gave Tony his old room. He had lunch and then took a lobby seat, looking across Hunt at the new bank. Stockmen, merchants and railroaders were filing in and out of it. Among them Tony saw Mark McCarron and the man had a frustrated look. By now he'd know that Margie had interceded for Tony Darrow.

A gunslung cowboy reined to a stop at the bank. He was Chuck Gleason and Tony saw him go to a teller's window over there. It meant that Chuck had drawn his pay at the Jaybird and was cashing the check.

Coming out of the bank Chuck crossed to join Tony in the hotel lobby. "It'll be all over town, *amigo*," he predicted, "before you can say 'don't shoot.' "

"Who'll tell it, Chuck?"

"Gabby Givens, naturally. Ever know Gabby to keep his mouth shut?"

"Never did," Tony agreed sadly. Givens, along with the entire Jaybird crew, had witnessed Amory's humiliating arrival. A chunky, good-natured rider, was Gabby, whose only fault was a wagging tongue.

"Nobody quit but me," Chuck reported. "Ed Murdy and the rest of 'em can't quite figure it out, but they're stringin' along with the boss."

"They put him to bed?"

"He didn't need putting to bed. Nothing much hurt but his feelings. Listen, kid, and get an earful. I quit and drew my time. But before I could saddle up, Blaise Amory himself lit out for town. I was only half a mile back of him all the way in."

"He keeps a room here at the Victoria," Tony said. "So he'll be showing up any minute."

"Guess again." Gleason grinned mysteriously. "I hit town right behind him and I saw him go into Brophy's Bar. 'Funny place for a fine gent like him!' thinks I. So I peek over the half-doors to see what the heck he wants in there."

Brophy's, Tony knew, was the toughest and most disorderly bar in town. Ranchfolk and railroaders rarely went in there. Usually the customers were nameless bad men and unemployed drifters. Its sawdust was well mixed with blood, men said, and there were bullet holes in the bar to prove it.

"What *did* he want?" Tony prodded.

"One rye whisky. That's all. I saw him down it. The joint was full of toughies, like it always is, but Amory didn't speak to any of 'em. He downed the slug and went out, climbed his horse and guess where he headed for?"

"Spengler's office over Easterday's store."

Chuck shook his head. "Believe it or not, he headed straight back to the Jaybird ranch. I followed him a mile or so to make sure."

That, Tony thought, didn't make sense. Why would Amory ride ten miles to town and then go home after a single drink? And even so why would he pick a dive like Brophy's?

"Put away your bronc, Chuck. Let's go look that joint over."

Shortly they were tramping west along Front, holster flaps open. "Could be he passed a signal, Chuck. Maybe he said something to the bartender when he ordered the drink."

"He paid for it with a dollar bill," Chuck remembered. "A note could be folded in the bill."

"A note maybe to Spengler," Tony amended. "Or to the guy who sniped Pancho Morales."

Beyond State Avenue they passed the Barlow and Sanderson stage station. From there on west about every fifth shop was a saloon and these got progressively more disreputable.

When they came to Brophy's Bar Tony looked in on a sawdust floor and a bar of unpainted pine. The backbar's mirror had flyspecks and a long diagonal crack. The bartender's hairless head and upturned mustaches made him look like a French barber. Brophy himself was merely a landlord and had nothing to do with operating the place. Tony looked the customers over. "A fine bunch of hoodlums!" he whispered. "Let's go in."

Chuck followed him in and almost at once they heard chairs scrape on the floor. Four card players near an open alley door had turned to face the newcomers. Each of the quartette wore a hip gun. One seemed to be a Spaniard and the other three were gringos. The three gringos had an air of shifty vigilance as though at any moment some old crime might catch up with them. Only the Spaniard was well dressed and well featured. The gringos looked like shabby, small-time thugs. At the near end of the bar a sheep-smelling derelict tried to panhandle a drink. He was cuffed and sent sprawling. Another customer guffawed and took a kick at him. There was no piano. Nothing but dirty sawdust and liquor fumes and evil men.

Tony took a place at midbar, Chuck siding him. "Keep an eye on those four ginks at the back table, Chuck. They seemed right interested when we walked in."

"I can see 'em in the bar mirror," Chuck said. He ordered rye and Tony took a small beer.

Tony held his glass critically to the light. In a loud voice he inquired, "Eusebio Sanchez been around here lately?"

"Don't know him." The barkeep's face looked convincingly blank.

"How about Blaise Amory? He been in lately?"

"I've heard of him, mister. But I don't know him by sight."

"What about that lawyer fella—Saul Spengler?"

This brought a harsh laugh. "Spengler? Give him two-bits and he'll be here in ten minutes."

Tony sipped his beer. The mirror told him that the four gunslung card players were alert and attentive. At least the three gringos were. One of them, a big burly man, whispered back of his hand to a pint-size man whose face had the sharpness of a rat's. The Spaniard, erect and more than commonly personable, picked up the cards and calmly shuffled them.

Tony tried one more question. "Pancho Morales used to come in here once in a while, didn't he?"

"Why not? Seein' as he was cook in the hashhouse next door." The bartender cocked an eye at Tony. "Who do you guys think you are, anyway? The census takers?"

A nudge from Chuck's elbow. "Rat-face sneaked out on us," he whispered. "He beat it out the alley door. Le's see where he goes."

They hurried out at the front. The man was sure to emerge from the alley either on San Juan Street or Edison. So Tony went one way and Chuck the other.

Edison Street was empty but when Tony followed it a block to Fifth he sighted both Chuck and Rat-face. The pint-size man had reached Fifth via San Juan and Chuck was trailing him. The man wore a narrow-brimmed brown hat with an undented crown. His forty-five gun looked incongruously big for him and sagged almost to his knee. "There he goes!" Chuck said as Tony caught up with him.

The man had darted up steps leading to offices over Easterday's grocery. Saul Spengler's shabby shingle marked the place.

"They're all tied in a knot," Tony concluded. "Spengler and Amory and the gang at Brophy's Bar."

"Shall we follow him up there?"

"No use, Chuck. Spengler would say the guy's a client and we can't prove he isn't. Let's wait across the street till he comes out."

It was a short wait. The small man came

scampering down to the walk. After hopping the town ditch, he hurried west to San Juan and turned right there. The cowboys followed cautiously at a distance.

This was a street of dwellings, most of them plank cottages. Beyond Third Street these thinned out and only a dirt path served for a sidewalk. Someone had planted cottonwood saplings along the street line. The small man, a block ahead, continued on.

Tony drew Chuck to a stop and they waited briefly. "Only one shack left ahead of him. Let's see if he turns in."

The shack was at the end of the street with a pile of sawdust by it. A portable mill had deserted the place after a season's setup to furnish lumber for the town. "He's stoppin' there," Chuck said.

The man had disappeared into the shack. Less than a minute later a thin gray smoke emerged from a stovepipe chimney. Then the man promptly reappeared and retraced his steps this way. "Duck," Chuck warned, and drew Tony back of a board fence.

The small man passed without seeing them, heading back toward Brophy's Bar. "Let's see what he set fire to," Chuck suggested. "It wasn't much, because the smoke's gone already."

They went on to the deserted millsite whose sawdust dump, no doubt, was now being used daily to furnish fresh footing in the town's saloons. The shack door had no lock and the glass of a window was broken. Inside they found a small monkey stove and two cots. Two kegs made seats at an upended packing box. Other cheap furnishings indicated that a pair of third-rate citizens had been batching here.

Tony opened the little stove and looked in. Filmy paper ashes there were still warm. Tony raked them out into a tin plate. "Look, Chuck. That gink walked clear out here just to burn a few papers."

"What kinda papers?"

"No way of telling . . . but hold on a minute. Here's a corner that didn't quite get burned." Tony took the scrap and held it to the light. Then he gave a low whistle. "It's the top corner of a letter, Chuck."

Enough of the letterhead was left to identify its source. It had been sent out by the United States Land Office at Del Norte.

9

When Tony awakened two mornings later his bedmate was gone. Chuck Gleason was now sharing his room at the Victoria. Tony shaved and went down to breakfast. In the dining room a cordial voice hailed him. “Hello there. Come and join me.”

Breakfasting alone was Receiver Guy Halderman from Del Norte. That he should be in Alamosa wasn’t strange, this being the biggest town in his territory. “Thanks, Mr. Halderman.” Tony took a seat at his table.

“I came down mainly to check on the Eusebio Sanchez case. And while I’m here I was hoping to see *you* again.” The little gray man smiled cryptically over the rim of his coffee cup.

“What about?”

“I offered you a job and you turned it down. After what’s happened, perhaps you’ll change your mind.”

Tony flushed a little. “Haven’t you changed yours, Mr. Halderman?” For surely the receiver had read news accounts of the recent inquests, and so would know that Tony had a prison record and that Mark McCarron had fired him.

“The fact still remains, Darrow, that you were recommended to me by Alva Adams. I respect his judgment. And since then you've been sponsored by someone else whose opinion rates high with me. She stopped by to see me on her way home with a sewing machine." A twinkle came to Halderman's brown eyes and crow's-feet spread from their corners.

Tony gaped. "You mean Helga Tarber?"

"Who else? So when the biggest merchant and the loveliest lady in the park both vouch for you, why should I hesitate about giving you a job?"

"She doesn't know anything about me," Tony said.

"It doesn't take a smart girl long," Halderman smiled, "to make up her mind about a man. Now about this job. A spy job you called it. My first idea was that you work from the inside—get on ranch payrolls to find out if the rancher was using pawns to file on adjacent lands."

"That's out now," Tony said grimly. "Most of the big outfits wouldn't take me on."

"So why not work from the *outside?*" The receiver narrowed his eyes thoughtfully. "You've homesteaded on the Conejos and we're approving your application. While you prove up you could work for the land office as a secret investigator, riding all over southwest Colorado on a hunt for fraudulent filings."

An idea flashed to Tony. "I'd do it on two conditions."

"Which are?"

"First, that I let a pal of mine in on it. Chuck Gleason. He's out of a job too and last night I talked him into filing a claim right next to mine." Tony added lightly and with a grin, "Case I get in a gunfight I might need Chuck to back me up."

"And your other condition?"

"That instead of checking filings next to ranches, you let me check any scattered filings where the applications came in the way Eusebio Sanchez' did."

The brown eyes squinted shrewdly. "The Sanchez application," Halderman remembered, "had four peculiarities. It came by mail. The attached filing fee wasn't a check or money order, but currency. The signature was made before the clerk of a distant county court. And the only address given by the applicant was a general delivery one. Your idea is to check on a list of parallel cases?"

"That's it. And we've got to keep an eye on this lawyer fella. Saul Spengler."

"Because you saw a land office envelope on Spengler's desk?"

"That's part of it. Most of it's because Spengler's tied up some way with four gyppers at Brophy's Bar. One of 'em ran to him for advice and then beat it home to burn up a land office letter."

A grim look came to Halderman as he stood up. "I'm going to pay a call on Spengler right now. We shouldn't be seen too much together, so you'd better not come along. I'll check with you before I leave town."

The receiver started out, then turned and sat down again. He looked at Tony Darrow with a personal and kindly sympathy. "I read what came out at the inquest," he said. "It's not hard to imagine how you feel about it. Is there any way I can help you?"

"Nothing could help me," Tony said, "except finding a man named Memphis Jack. I don't know him by any other name."

"Tell me about him," Halderman invited.

"He was a crony of the Tolliver brothers. He'd show up about once a year and stay overnight with us. Last time he was there I came back from some chore and heard him giving Podge Tolliver the dickens about something. He said: 'You're playing with fire, Podge; you and Ferg better quit it before you get burnt.' And Podge said: 'Pipe down; here comes the kid.' "

Halderman weighed it shrewdly. "From that you conclude that Memphis Jack was advising the Tollivers to stop stealing horses, and that Podge was warning Jack not to let the kid, yourself, hear them talk about it. Is that all?"

"Not quite. Just before he left that day Memphis Jack asked me when I'd be eighteen years old. I said in a coupla months. He said, 'If you're smart, kid, you'll go straight to the nearest recruiting office and join the army.' "

Halderman nodded. "Sounds like he was trying to get you away from there, before the Tollivers got into trouble."

"I didn't figure it out," Tony said, "till I was serving my term. When I got out I went straight to Memphis. I'd heard Jack mention a bar there. I found the bar and the barman said Memphis Jack was the only name he knew for the man. He said Jack had left owing him five dollars and later had sent the money by mail, from Alamosa, Colorado."

"A man who pays a debt when he doesn't have to," Halderman offered, "is fundamentally honest. You came to this county looking for Jack?"

Tony nodded. "Can't locate him anywhere. Maybe he's gone on to California."

Halderman made a note of the name. "I'll check the records of the land department for a man named John from Tennessee. Let's not give up on him yet, Tony." The receiver smiled and went out.

And Tony, as the morning advanced, waited restlessly in the lobby. It was nearly noon when Chuck Gleason came in and beckoned him aside. "I've been askin' about those gazaboes at Brophy's Bar."

"Find out anything?"

"Little squirt we followed goes by the name

of Pinky Mock. Other three call themselves Wycross, Huggins and Sandoval."

"What do they do for a living?"

"*Quien sabe*? If I had my guess I'd say Huggins and Mock roll drunks and rob stages. The big guy, Wycross, is a smoothie with soft hands. Notice those flat, glassy eyes of his. Diego Sandoval's a cut above the others. Dealt faro down at Taos, one time. Huggins killed a man, about six months back, down at China Pete's. They call him Trigger Huggins."

"Fine, upstanding gents! Who told you all this?"

"Dayman at Blackmore's barn, on Denver Street. They keep their broncs there."

"What brands?"

"All different. As far as the barnman knows, none of 'em ever worked for a park ranch."

"For you, mister." A hotel-boy handed Tony a sealed envelope.

The message was from Guy Halderman and said:

> Spengler's office is empty. He was seen boarding a train for Pueblo last night. When he comes back let me know. I'm driving home to Del Norte now. You're hired on the terms mentioned, but you may confide in no one but your friend Gleason. A list of land filings which meet

the four conditions we discussed will be mailed to you at once.

G. H.

Tony read it aloud to Chuck. And when Chuck looked confused he summed up: "We stuck a pin in something at Brophy's Bar. We mention four names—Sanchez, Amory, Spengler, Morales. Right away Pinky Mock scoots to Spengler for advice. Spengler tells him to burn a land office paper. Then Spengler himself does a fadeout."

After lunch Chuck Gleason filled out a homestead application blank. It described a quarter section adjacent to Tony's. "First time I'm at the courthouse," Chuck said, "I'll sign it and mail it in."

A buckboard went by with Margie McCarron driving. It stopped at Ada Bowers' millinery shop and Tony hurried that way. Margie had just tied her team when he caught up.

The way she looked at him made the grin go dry on his face. Her eyes blazed and her words cut. "I'm ashamed of you, Tony Darrow!" He could only assume she was accepting Blaise Amory's version of the fight.

"I'd be a heap more ashamed of myself," Tony said, "if I was working for Amory. He told you all about it, I guess."

"Gabby Givens told us . . . and I couldn't

believe it was true. So I rode over and asked Blaise. . . . How could you be so ungrateful? After he stood up for you and offered you a job . . ." A righteous indignation fired Margie and her tone was scathing. "It just means father was right, after all." She brushed by Tony to enter the shop but he caught up with her at the door, barring the way.

"Look, Margie. You heard Amory's side of this, now listen to mine. The truth is I didn't touch that fella till he tried to kill me with his brute of a horse."

She stared up at him. "But why," she protested, "would he do that? He had nothing but good will for you. He went to you when you were in trouble and tried to help. He . . ."

"He tried to kill me," Tony broke in. His temper had snapped, now.

Margie recoiled a step, her stare uncompromising. "You expect me to believe that? I knew Blaise long before I knew you, Tony Darrow."

"You didn't know him six years ago," Tony blurted, "when he ran to the Fort Garland barracks with a story about Ute Indians."

"What difference does it make," she retorted, "whether I knew him then?"

"Because there weren't any Indians. That job was pulled by a gang of cutthroat whites and Amory was in on it. He's a black-hearted killer with enough blood on his hands to float a boat."

For a moment the enormity of the charge robbed her of movement and speech. When words came there was no scorn in them, just a sorrowful disillusionment. "How stupid I've been, all this year when I thought you were . . . well . . . somebody nice to know! But you're not. You're low and cheap and contemptible, Tony Darrow. And please don't ever speak to me again."

She went past him and into the shop. Tony knew better than to follow. He went bitterly up the walk and circled the block looking for Chuck. Passing a knot of men he heard his own name and Amory's mentioned. The talk stopped as he came near. Clearly his run-in with Amory was spreading all over the range. The *Independent* would make hot copy of it.

He was walking west along Front when the paper's editor ran him down. Questions volleyed. The editor knew what the Jaybird crew had seen and heard, nothing more. "Anything to add, Darrow?"

"Plenty." Tony smiled mirthlessly. "But I'm goin' to let you dig it up from a Ute named Unahwa. He's around somewhere."

"Unahwa? A Ute?" The editor wrote the name on his pad. "What's *he* got to do with it?"

"Find him and ask him. When you do you'll get one whale of a yarn." Tony elbowed past the man and went on up Front. Chuck, he reasoned, might be nosing around Brophy's Bar to keep an eye on Pinky Mock's playmates. So Tony continued on to Brophy's.

The swinging half-doors bulged open and a man toppled out, landing in a heap on the walk. "Get out and stay out," a voice boomed from the doorway, and Tony saw the bartender there. The house had just bounced an undesirable customer.

This one picked himself up. He had a haggard, drink-starved face and Tony felt a pang of pity for this human lump of filth and rags. A glance into Brophy's told him Chuck wasn't there. Otherwise the scene was the same as before. The inmates looked tough enough to avoid on dark nights. Stale smells filled the place and trash-littered sawdust covered the floor. Four card players at a back table were, if Chuck had them tabbed correctly, Wycross, Mock, Huggins and Sandoval.

Nothing was to be gained by tangling with them. Tony backed out and turned east along the walk.

A tug at his sleeve stopped him. At his elbow stood the down-and-outer he'd just seen booted from Brophy's Bar. This was a touch, Tony supposed, for the price of a drink. The man's question, huskily cautious, surprised him. "Your name Darrow?"

"Yeh. Why?"

The man looked warily over his shoulder. "You had a run-in with Blaise Amory?"

"That's right. How do *you* know about it?"

"People in bars talk," the man said in a hoarse whisper. "I got eyes in my head even if I ain't got a dime in my pants. What about the price of a ticket to Pueblo?"

So it was a touch after all! A ticket to Pueblo would cost several dollars. This man hailed from there, probably, and was now stranded in Alamosa—his one idea being to get back to old haunts where bartenders were likely to be more sympathetic.

"You saw something at Brophy's," Tony prodded. "And you'd spill it for a ticket to Pueblo?"

The shifty eyes peered both ways along the walk. "Not here," the man warned. "In the depot ticket room." With a beckoning nod he scurried off in that direction.

Tony followed at a distance. He decided to gamble. Maybe this bum really knew something.

No train was due and the depot waiting room was empty. Tony found the man waiting in nervous eagerness. At the ticket window he bought a one-way fare to Pueblo. "It's yours," he promised the outcast, "after you deliver. Not before. Start talking."

"Couldn't you throw in a pint of red-eye?" the man begged. "It's a long ride over the hill."

"No red-eye. Talk or I'll tear up the ticket."

"I was in Brophy's the other day," the man

confided, “when Amory came in. He didn’t say nothin’ to nobody. He just ordered rye, tossed it down and went out.”

“I knew that already,” Tony said. It checked exactly with Chuck Gleason’s observation.

“But as he went out,” the man added, “he flipped away his cigaret. It lit in the sawdust right close to Trigger Huggins and I seen Huggins pick it up.”

“What did Huggins do with it?” Tony was sharply alert now.

“It was a long snipe, with only a few puffs gone from it. Huggins unrolled it, looked at the paper, then burned it.”

“What would he do that for?”

The man’s rheumy eyes slitted. “Maybe he read a name on it. Maybe it was *your* name, mister.”

“Why would Amory flip my name to Trigger Huggins?”

“It happened before, mister. A week ago Saturday night. I was there and I seen this same Amory come in. He tossed down a rye and flipped away a snipe as he went out. And I seen Trigger Huggins pick it up.”

“Well?”

“Then I seen Trigger duck out. ’Bout a hour later I heard a shot down around State and Front. Purty soon the bar was buzzin’. Fella named Pancho Morales, they said, had been rifled from the dark.”

10

"It's as simple as that," Tony explained to Chuck Gleason at the hotel. "Whenever Blaise Amory wants anyone knocked off, he orders rye at Brophy's and then flips a snipe to Huggins."

"Slow up," Chuck objected with a confused look. "You're 'way ahead of me."

"It makes sense," Tony insisted, "if Amory's top rod in a gang that's been operating a long time. The same gang that wiped out the Arragon party six years ago. What devilment they're up to now we don't know. But if anybody gets in its way he has to be knocked off. Amory gives the signal for it, by code at Brophy's."

That was Monday. On Tuesday Chuck Gleason rode to the courthouse at Conejos. On Wednesday he returned to report that the clerk of the county court had attested his homestead application and that he'd mailed it to the Del Norte land office. "It's the quarter section right upcreek from yours, Tony, and I drove me a stake there on my way back."

"I'll toss you," Tony offered, "to see which claim we build a cabin on first. Yours or mine."

"Heads." Chuck tossed a coin and it settled with the eagle up. "So we build first on *your* claim, Tony. All we need now is some *dinero*."

Cabin, shed and corral would cost close to a thousand dollars and Tony had no idea where he could get a sum like that. His surprise came on Thursday when McNeil of the new bank sent for him.

Tony went there at once. A dazed look rode his face when he recrossed Hunt Avenue to join Chuck at the hotel. "We're rich, cowboy! Take a look." Tony tossed Chuck a bank book which showed that a thousand dollars had been placed to his credit. "And all I had to do was sign a note!"

Chuck gaped. "You mean they don't believe what it says here?" He'd been reading today's issue of the *Independent* which told all about Tony's clash with Blaise Amory. Amory's version of it was naturally the one reported, since Tony had offered none of his own. "Darrow evades discussion," the story said, "by hinting the existence of an Indian witness named Unahwa. If such a witness exists, the *Independent* is unable to find him."

"Whether they believe it or not," Tony said jubilantly, "those bankers were plenty friendly when I went in there. 'Good morning, Mr. Darrow,' they said. 'We understand you've filed on land and want to improve it. Will a thousand dollars be enough, Mr. Darrow?' "

Chuck whistled. Then a shrewd gleam came to his eyes. "All it means, *amigo*, is they've decided you told the truth at them inquests. So they're plumb grateful to you for stoppin' Tully and Wager from stickin' 'em up."

"They didn't mention Tully or Wager," Tony said, "or the wagon haul from Del Norte. With most folks on this range the vote's ten to one I made it all up. You heard any new talk around town, Chuck?"

Gleason licked a cigaret. "Only that purty near everybody's sidin' with Amory. The wise word is you're sore at him for beatin' your time with Margie McCarron. So you just pulled him off his bronc and pistol-whipped him."

A brakeman came across from the depot. Tony knew him by sight and remembered the man's run. It was the night passenger run to Pueblo, and back on alternate nights.

"Wait a minute, Chuck," Tony said. He got up and followed the brakeman, who'd gone back to the hotel lunch counter for a cup of coffee. Perching on the next stool he asked, "Do you know Saul Spengler?"

The railroader gave a cock-eyed stare. "Sure. But I'm not braggin' about it."

"Remember seein' him leave here on your train Sunday night?"

"Yeh, I remember." Puzzlement narrowed the man's eyes. "Conductor and I worried about him a little, that trip. He had a bottle of hooch and was hittin' it in the smoker. When we missed him at La Veta we were afraid maybe he'd got high and fell off. But I guess he didn't, or a section gang would've found him on the track."

"You missed him at La Veta? I thought he went all the way to Pueblo."

"He was supposed to. He had a ticket there. But when we stopped on the pass to unhook the pusher, he wasn't aboard. Must've got off at Fort Garland or Placer. Those are the only stops we make between here and the top."

"Is that the last you saw of him?"

The brakeman nodded. "If he came back to Alamosa it wasn't on my run. Likely he's still at Placer or Garland."

Tony went back to Chuck, brooding over it. Placer was a mining town with seven saloons and a thousand people. Also it had a turntable where the railroad put on a pusher for the climb to La Veta. Garland was an army post halfway between Alamosa and Placer. What would that booze hound of a notary be doing at either place?

"Looks like he ducked out to keep from being questioned," Tony said. "Guess I'll go tell Milt Yeager where he is."

He took a walk up to State Avenue and found the undersheriff in his office. But after hearing about Saul Spengler, Yeager only yawned. "It's a free country, ain't it? No crime if he took a train ride to Placer."

"No," Tony admitted. "But the killing of

Morales on your doorstep was a crime and you haven't nicked it yet. A land office paper ties Morales to Sanchez and the envelope it came in ties Sanchez to Spengler. Then when Receiver Halderman comes down here to ask questions, Spengler does a fadeout. Pretends he's going to Pueblo but gets off either at Garland or Placer."

Yeager shifted uncomfortably. "What you want me to do, cowboy?"

"Let's find out if Spengler intends to come back. A quick look at his office oughta tell us that."

Yeager agreed with a shrug. He went out and Tony followed him to Easterday's store. Easterday had keys to rooms on the second floor and Yeager borrowed one of them. Tony tagged along up the dusty steps.

The notary's office was just as he'd last seen it. A litter on table and desk. Empty liquor bottles. Law books, musty and long unused. Cobwebs festooned from the ceiling. An anteroom had a washstand and an iron bed. Shabby garments were strewn about. There was nothing to indicate that Spengler had left for good.

Yeager sifted through the desk litter. But it was Tony whose roving eye missed something. A thing which had been prominent on his last visit here. He searched the desk for it and even rummaged through boxes in the bunkroom.

"He took it with him," Tony concluded.

Yeager gave a vacant stare. "Took *what* with him?"

"His notary seal."

The fact didn't impress Yeager. He locked the office and returned the key downstairs. Tony walked with him to the corner.

"Got yourself a job yet, cowboy?" Yeager's tone seemed curious rather than sympathetic. He was known to be a friend of Blaise Amory.

"I've staked myself a homestead," Tony evaded. "Got to build a cabin on it. Know where I can find a good cabin contractor?"

"Bill Epps has some cabin timber on hand," Yeager remembered. "You might talk to him. Lives on the river bank 'bout four mile below here."

A round trip to Epps' place would fill out the day. Tony went to the livery barn and saddled up. The saddle had a carbine in its scabbard and he checked the loads.

In the heat of midafternoon he made dust down East Front, past China Pete's red-lamped doorway, and hit the river just beyond. He followed the south bank along a rutted wagon trail. The Rio Grande, its current alternating between shallow riffles and unfordable cascades, ran at his left; while to the right a sagebrush bottomland reached to the piny slope of the San Juans.

A treeless valley except for thin lines of cottonwood and willow along its streams. Fertile land most of which was still unclaimed. For the typical homeseeker, wheeling over Mosca Pass with all the park spread out before him, had been inclined to choose a spot on the park's edges rather than in its middle. From its edges gushed the mountain streams of clear trout water; around its edges ran a forest alive with game; there fuel and water were certain even in the driest years. While here in the valley's open center rainfall was light, averaging less than seven inches a year. Many of the mountain streams, Tony knew, sank into sands and disappeared before reaching the park's main artery, the Rio Grande. So most of the homesteads filed thus far were miles away from the river, at the fringe of the park's timbered walls, as was the Phineas Tarber place above Del Norte.

The thought reminded Tony of Helga Tarber. He wondered if she'd read about his trouble with Blaise Amory.

At the Epps place he found Bill Epps holding an axe to a pedal grindstone. The man had been a carpenter at Placer, had helped build the hotel there. Now he was proving up a quarter section here but spent half his time building cabins in Alamosa.

The one he'd built for himself looked good to Tony. "Mind if I see the inside?"

"Help yourself." Epps waved a hand and went on with his grinding.

Tony went into the cabin and made an inspection. The walls were pine slabs with the bark side out. There were two rooms and a lean-to kitchen. The floors were pine boards and one room had built-in bunks. The roof was gabled and shingled. Each room had a glass window and one of them had a stone fireplace. Nothing was painted or varnished but every crack was expertly chinked. Compared with the usual settler's sod-roof shanty, this was a palace.

"How much," Tony asked, "to build me one just like it providin' I furnish a man to help?"

"Depends on where it is," Epps said.

"It's on the Conejos River 'bout two miles above the old Pike stockade."

"That's six miles," Epps calculated, "from where I got my cabin timber stacked."

"The man I furnish, meaning either myself or Chuck Gleason, could do the hauling. And anything else you want him to do."

"What about a shed and corral?"

"Just figure on the main house. I can throw up a shed and corral later."

"Five hundred dollars," Epps proposed.

"It's a deal. You'll find Chuck or me there any day, after tomorrow. Come as soon as you can." Tony shook hands and rode back toward town.

He'd ridden about half of the four miles when his hat bounced. He felt the bounce before he heard the shot. It came from a willow thicket across the river.

On this bank there were no willows. But Tony had passed a growth of cottonwoods a hundred yards back. He wheeled his calico and raced to them, jerking carbine from scabbard. There was a hole in his hat. He knew it without looking. And the sniper had a rifle.

The same rifle, Tony was willing to bet, which had done for Pancho Morales. Morales had been a stationary target and so there'd been no miss. On a trotting horse Tony had made a more difficult shot.

No use firing back till he had cover. He came to the screen of cottonwoods and there he spurred down to the river's edge, hoping to ford and close in on the sniper. But this stretch of water was a rocky cascade—an uncrossable torrent. Tony took off his hat, looked at the holes there, slapped it back on with a surge of anger. He remembered a cigaret tossed away at Brophy's Bar. And Huggins who'd picked it up just before the gunning of Morales!

And Blaise Amory who, after a thrashing by Tony Darrow, had raced hotfoot to repeat that signal at Brophy's!

A fever to close in on the sniper flamed in Tony's brain. An immediate obstacle was the cascading Rio Grande and he rode down its brink to find an easier crossing. When he came to less turbulent water he plunged in there.

In midstream the calico floundered, belly deep, but Tony bullied him to the far bank. Here were willows and Tony pushed grimly upstream through them. Mosquitoes buzzed. Switches slapped his face and left welts there.

He came tardily to the place from which the shot had been fired. An empty Winchester shell marked it, and the tracks of a horse. Hoofprints which had arrived from the direction of town and which led back the same way. After his miss, the killer had raced for Alamosa.

Tony followed the tracks to a spot just below the railroad bridge. There they crossed to the other side and he lost them in the dust of Front Street. He rode bitterly up Front, past rack after rack of tethered horses. Many of the mounts showed the sweat of hard riding. Most of them had rifles in the scabbards. Almost any one of them could be the mount of Trigger Huggins. Or Huggins could unsaddle at some barn and go on afoot to his regular stand, Brophy's Bar.

Tony lost no time getting there himself. His temper was still boiling as he swung to the walk in front of Brophy's. A dozen idlers saw him dismount there, rifle in hand, and push through twin half-doors into the barroom.

Of those inside, only the barkeeper immediately noticed his entrance. Bar customers had their backs to Tony. An alley door stood open and near it was a table with four card players. The same four—Wycross, Huggins, Mock and Diego Sandoval. One of the four, Tony knew at once, had just arrived. Three had dry boots. But the boots of Trigger Huggins were wet to the ankles, proving he'd just forded a stirrup-deep river. Also he was buying chips in a game which, judging from unequal stacks in front of the other three, had been going on for some time.

All four men were hatted but Huggins' hat had the tallest crown. A spot of green caught in the band looked like a willow leaf. It wasn't proof and a sense of frustration flogged Tony. Here was a man who'd just tried to kill him from ambush—and yet there was no use in even taking the tale to Yeager. Huggins would deny it and the other three would swear him alibis. And next time Tony rode the range there'd come another bullet from the brush.

Suddenly Tony realized the bartender was looking at him. And that he hadn't produced a shotgun from under the bar. If he were an ally of the Huggins gang he'd at least call their attention to Tony's rifle-armed intrusion. Instead he only wore a look of detached interest.

Tony advanced three steps down the sawdust floor. He stopped with the rifle hanging loose and horizontal in his hands, but with the barrel pointing at Huggins' head. Here at least was a chance to see how much stuff these fellows had.

Each of them wore a gun; but they were seated and their hands were busy with cards.

"Still looking for me, Huggins?" Tony's abrupt question made all heads snap around to face him.

Huggins dropped his cards and gave a frozen stare. The muzzle of a rifle stared back and Tony said, quietly this time, "Here I am, Hug, if you still want me."

For half a minute no sound came. Not even a whisper. Boldness had its sway in this company of cheap men, most of them ready to fawn on any courage superior to their own. Silence too from the bartender, who would certainly intervene if aligned with Huggins and Sandoval. Tony advanced another step, his hip-high rifle pointed at Huggins' head. Some of the reckless fury oozed out of him when he saw how really craven these men were. In its place came an impulse to mock them, and to make them lose face before this barful of men.

"That's right, Trigger. Keep your hands in a safe place. Wycross, you got the right idea too. Just keep your hands on the table and your eyes on the hole in my hat."

Every eye in the room went to the hole in Tony's hat. "Trigger put it there," Tony told them. "Missed me just this far." He squeezed a trigger and his rifle cracked. A tall-crowned hat bounced on the head of Trigger Huggins. Every eye in the room jerked to it, and to a bullet hole which had just appeared there. A fish-belly pallor rode Huggins' face.

It was the same with the big, flat-eyed Wycross and with the midget, Pinky Mock. Only the Mexican remained swarthily nerveless. Tony heard quick-drawn breaths all about him. When a rifle was held only belt-high it took uncanny skill to shoot with such accuracy.

Tony sensed that most of the room, for this passing moment at least, was with him. He took a chance. "Any of you guys wanta earn four-bits? You can do it easy enough. Just come and tell me the next time Blaise Amory orders rye in here and flips his cigaret to Trigger Huggins."

A faint snicker came from somewhere. Wycross, Mock and Huggins sat in petrified panic staring at the muzzle of a rifle. But the Spaniard brought a sack and papers from his shirt pocket and rolled a cigaret. As he licked the flap he gazed with a calm insolence at Tony.

Tony met his eyes and grinned. "Maybe I owe you an apology, Diego. For a minute I had you tagged yellow, like these gringos."

Sandoval blew a smoke ring and said coolly, "I have no fear of you, señor."

Tony's grin widened. "So I notice."

"But some day I will kill you, señor." Diego Sandoval picked up the cards and began laying out a game of solitaire. He ignored Tony and the entire barroom with superb *sang froid.*

They wouldn't shoot him in the back, Tony reasoned. Not in front of so many witnesses. So he turned and walked out through the street door.

11

The Tarbers, for many generations in Vermont, had been deeply religious. And since transplanting himself to a Colorado wilderness Phineas Tarber hadn't changed. On a Sunday in June, as usual, he and Helga attended church in Del Norte.

At noon the service ended and the small congregation emerged to visit a bit by the tie racks. Phineas and Helga didn't linger long. There were chores to do at the ranch.

Often they came in by buggy but today they'd come by saddle. Helga's was a side saddle, since her church skirt was ground length. Weekdays she rode astride in denims. She led her horse to a block and mounted from it. A dozen young men were clearly aware of the graceful figure she made, seated sidewise there. A few of them had gone courting to the little ranch on San Francisco Creek; others wanted to, but were a little awed by the austerity of Phineas Tarber.

"Come, daughter." Phineas spurred his horse up the street. The girl cantered after him and they took the trail for home.

"Mr. Halderman spoke to me at church, father."

No answer from Phineas.

"He asked if I'd seen Tony Darrow. Why would he be interested in Tony Darrow?"

When her father still didn't respond, Helga's voice gave up but her mind didn't. For more than a month the Alamosa weekly, to which they subscribed, had been full of Tony Darrow. Tony's exposure as a one-time convict. His discharge from the McCarron ranch. His fight with Blaise Amory. And finally a scene in some Front Street barroom where, according to many witnesses, he'd dared to link Blaise Amory with the very lowest of its low-lived customers.

All of which confused Helga. What she'd personally seen of Tony Darrow made her like him. Yet what she'd *heard* of him, via news accounts and street talk, made him into a cross between an ex-outlaw and a barroom brawler. Most of his old friends, they said, had turned cold shoulders. Even Margie McCarron. And Helga, that day at the Perry House, had sensed a more than ordinary attachment between Tony and Margie. Yet forced to take sides either with Blaise Amory or Tony Darrow, the Wagon Wheel girl had chosen Amory.

I wouldn't, Helga thought, but had no idea why she wouldn't. She'd met Amory only once and Tony but twice. How could she fairly take sides? One of them, obviously, had lied about the fight on the Conejos. A common rumor was that Tony had lied out of spite, to discredit Amory with Margie McCarron. Yet a few still believed in Tony. One was Guy Halderman. Another was the bank at Alamosa; for word had leaked out about the bank lending Tony money on his bare note. Tony who didn't even have a job!

Or did he? He was constantly in the saddle, people said, riding hither and yon through the park. He'd popped up at remote ranches and homesteads all the way from Wagon Wheel Gap to San Luis; and from Saguache to Cumbres Pass. He'd been seen on far trails, in the hills near Mosca where the great dunes sang by moonlight. The mystery of the man intrigued Helga. Another cowboy had joined him in filing a pair of homesteads on the lower Conejos—at the very spot of the Arragon massacre of '74. A massacre from which a single hero had emerged, Blaise Amory, with a mantle of glamour and the stature of a paladin.

All of this absorbed Helga on the homeward ride with her father. The six miles took them an hour, making it one o'clock when they dismounted at the barn. Before Helga could uncinch her saddle girth she noticed something. "You left the corral gate open, father."

The gate stood open and a team of fine mules was gone. Buckie and Benny. Helga had watered them before leaving for church.

"I did *not* leave it open," Phineas said. He rode to the open gate and looked at the ground there. Just outside of it was a plowed garden area which he'd dragged smooth only yesterday. Hoofprints could now be seen in the garden soil and Phineas followed them a little way.

He came loping back with a granite-grim face. He rushed into the house and came out with a rifle. By then Helga had stripped the side saddle from her horse and had stalled the animal.

"The mules were stolen," Phineas announced bluntly, "while we were at church."

"Are you sure, father?"

"They were led away, not driven." Phineas pointed to a corral post. "Two halters I left hanging there are gone. The tracks are close together. Two horses and two mules. One horseman led the mules."

Helga looked at him in dismay. The missing halters admitted no other conclusion.

"Stay here, Helga," Phineas commanded. He rode southward along the tracks of two horses and two mules.

Despair possessed Helga. He looked so hopelessly inadequate in his black go-to-church coat and his flat Sunday hat, from which there'd been no time to change. And suppose he caught up with his precious mules! What chance would he have in a fight with outlaws?

His rifle, Helga knew, was an old 1866 model rimfire forty-four. Nine years ago, in '71, he'd used it to stand off marauding Utes until Fort Garland cavalry had arrived to disperse them. At the time Helga had been only eleven, too young to own a firearm. Four years later Phineas had presented her with an up-to-date center-fire repeater which had infinitely superior ballistics. Rimfire weapons had since then become practically obsolete. Everyone now used the 1873 model center-fire 44-40s.

Everyone, that is, but her old-fashioned father. The horse thieves he now chased would certainly have center-fire weapons, and with them could shoot twice as far and twice as accurately. Phineas Tarber wouldn't have a chance.

A tightness clutched Helga's throat as she raced for the house. In ten minutes she was out again dressed in her work clothes—denim pants, wool shirt and buckskin jacket. In hand was her own center-fire 44-40 with which for the last four falls she'd helped her father bring in elk for winter meat.

She saddled up again, choosing a standard stock saddle with a scabbard flapping its right skirt. Helga tightened the cinches, shoving her rifle into the boot. Her father's battered work hat hung on a barn peg. As an afterthought the girl pulled it down over her yellow hair. From a distance she and her father would now appear as two men and this, she hoped dimly, might make the thieves abandon the mules rather than turn and fight.

Helga loped southward along a line of shod prints. Her father was out of sight, miles ahead of her by now. Presently she curbed her impatience and reined to a slower pace. Her father, and even the fugitive outlaws, would do the same. No long race had ever been won by winding mounts.

She crossed Nicodemes Gulch and struck Raton Creek just below Raton Park. The creek here had a small flow which would sink into sands before reaching the Rio Grande. The upland to Helga's right was timbered while the flatland to her left was sage. The tracks of flight skirted the edge of the timber and kept generally south, toward New Mexico.

Beyond Raton Creek the girl sighted her father, half a mile ahead. Pressing on she caught up with him at Dry Creek. He twisted sternly in his saddle. "Go back, Helga."

"Only if you do," she said stubbornly. It was the first time she'd ever disobeyed Phineas Tarber.

"Then stay well behind me," he said angrily. This she did, at about three lengths. When he walked his mount she walked hers. When he spurred to a trot she kept the same gait.

Soon the tracks veered to the right into pine and aspen known as Rock Creek Park. To Helga the reason was clear. A few settlers lived along Rock Creek and the thieves were taking care not to be seen in flight leading two mules. The tracks kept just inside the tree lines, emerging into the open again at the toe of Greenie Mountain.

From here Helga could see nearly all of San

Luis Park—its wide saggy floor with the town of Alamosa centering it, and on beyond to the snowy Sangre de Cristos. Forty miles to her left the dunes of singing sands reared a thousand feet above the sage.

"I must catch them before nightfall," Phineas muttered; he rode resolutely on.

They crossed Fulcher Gulch, dry and treeless, and came to Gato Creek where there was a trickle of water and a shelter of scrub aspen. Phineas stopped, warily, because plainly the thieves had also halted here.

Fresh ashes indicated that a fire had been kindled within the hour. Warm too was a can in which the fugitives had made coffee. Helga's quick eye saw a few grains of oats, slobbered from the mouths of horses.

"They're going a long way," Phineas concluded. And Helga also knew that men who travel far and fast must grain their mounts. A twenty-minute stop for that purpose would pay dividends in speed.

"We've no grain for ours," the girl argued, "so we'll never catch them. Please let's turn back, father."

"What! And give up the best span of mules in the park?" Phineas resumed the pursuit doggedly and Helga no less stubbornly followed.

They'd now come perhaps fifteen miles and the afternoon was late. Nightfall would force them to stop. By then they wouldn't be far from Conejos, the county seat, where at least they could report to a sheriff.

The sun dipped as they rode on, at last sinking back of the San Juans. But there'd be two hours of twilight in which to read prints. Helga hoped they'd pass without an encounter. She wanted her mules, but she wanted still more to keep her father out of an unequal fight.

It was in the last hour of light when they sighted Alamosa Creek. Its cottonwoods, now in full leaf, made a course of green trailing down from upland pine to lowland sage. Helga looked a few miles downcreek and saw the roofs of a ranch. The Wagon Wheel, she knew. Margie McCarron lived there; and a crew of riders.

Why not race to the ranch and recruit help? Ranch hands were always ready and eager to chase horse thieves.

To suggest this Helga spurred abreast of her father. Then something whistled past her and a second later, from the cottonwoods ahead, came the crack of a rifle. Another whirr was followed by the same distant sound. "Dismount, Helga!" Phineas shouted. "Get back of a rock."

He slid to the ground and pulled her from her saddle. She saw two puffs of smoke at the Alamosa Creek cottonwoods, about four hundred yards ahead. A bullet kicked sand at her feet. Helga snatched the rifle from her saddle boot, dropped to all fours and crawled for cover.

Only one sizable boulder was close by and Phineas made Helga lie prone back of it. He himself dived for a hummock of sand to her left. Aiming his old rimfire over it he fired at the next puff of smoke.

Helga herself fired and saw a dry bough drop from a limb just over her target. She'd at least let them know they were fighting two guns.

Another slug from the creek brush dashed sand over Phineas. His cover was inadequate and he darted for another, a higher hummock a few strides away.

Midway to it he staggered, dropped the rifle. Helga saw him go to his knees, hands clutching his midriff, and then topple forward with a groan. Helga ran to him and kneeled over him. "Father!" He didn't answer and she saw a redness spread on his shirt. As another bullet whirred by, a fury possessed her. She stood erect, rifle at her cheek, and pumped six fast shots at smoke puffs along the creek. The last trigger pull brought only a click. Helga dropped the empty rifle and took her father by the shoulders. Inch by inch she dragged him to the higher hummock of sand.

A bullet had passed between two ribs a little lower, she thought, than the right lung. In an agony of despair Helga took off her jacket, used a knife to slash the lining from it. Then she removed her father's coat—the long black church coat in which he'd worshiped only this morning—and from that too she ripped the lining.

From the two linings she made strips and wound them around his body—around and around until she'd staunched the blood. He was conscious. And a little of the old sternness was still on his lips. "I told you not to come," he rebuked faintly.

Then she became aware there'd been no firing since her own fusillade of six rapid shots. She looked toward the creek and on higher ground far beyond it saw two retreating horsemen. One of them led two haltered mules. They were more than half a mile away, fading in dim, gray twilight.

For that much as least she could be thankful. She leaned tenderly over Phineas and kissed his lips. "There's a ranch downcreek, father. I'll bring help from there, and a doctor. You just lie right still and wait."

It wrenched her to desert him even briefly, but there was no other way. Helga made a pillow for his head. "I'll be back real soon," she promised, then stepped into her saddle and rode hard toward the Wagon Wheel ranch.

In the cool dusk of a June Sunday, Mark McCarron sat comfortably on his porch, chewing an unlighted cigar. A soft breeze brought him the scent of alfalfa, now just coming to bloom in his meadow. Red and white dots beyond were Herefords which had wintered in good flesh. McCarron eyed them complacently. A colt kicked up heels in the corral and down by the bunkhouse four of his hands had just finished a game of horseshoes.

Life had become pleasant for Mark McCarron. Through the open window came gay voices, the sound of fingers tripping over piano keys. Margie and Blaise Amory were in there. Blaise hadn't missed a Sunday call for six weeks and this had lifted a great weight from McCarron's heart and mind. He need no longer worry about Tony Darrow.

Until May, Tony had been a problem. Margie's pretty red head had, McCarron suspected, been full of him and she'd talked about him entirely too much. This hadn't at all suited McCarron, whose choice from the first had been Blaise Amory. Blaise was a man of solid prospects who'd go high and far—perhaps to the governorship some day. The idea of Margie passing him up for a common cowboy had been more than distressing.

Yet there'd been no decent excuse to fire Tony—no way to get him off the ranch and out of Margie's life.

No way until that sudden break at the Perry House dance on the first of May. Tony an ex-convict! A made-to-order excuse for letting him go, thus removing him from daily contacts with Margie, and McCarron had snatched at it.

Nor had he any regrets. After all it was best for Margie. Things were working out fine now between her and Blaise. As for Tony Darrow, he'd convicted himself by outbursts of jealousy-inspired charges against a rival.

Pounding hoofbeats turned McCarron's head toward the upcreek pasture. A rider was coming at a breakneck pace. A frown furrowed the rancher's brow. These reckless young cowboys shouldn't treat a horse like that!

When this one drew up McCarron got to his feet, blinking. It wasn't a man but a girl. "I need help, please!" she announced breathlessly. "My father has been shot. . . ."

Before she'd finished, the frantic distress in her voice had drawn Margie and Amory from the house. "You're Helga Tarber!" Margie's sympathy was no less swift than her recognition. Four cowboys, led by the Wagon Wheel's capable young foreman, Luke Priddy, came running from the bunkhouse. It was Margie who took urgent command. "Sam, ride fast to Alamosa for Doctor Gale." . . . "Luke, hitch up the spring wagon and take the seat out." . . . "Bud, put a mattress in the bed of it." Margie stood at Helga's stirrup, reached up to squeeze her hand. "We'll take care of everything, Helga. Just tell us where he is. . . ."

"I'll take you there," Helga insisted. They

couldn't make her dismount. By now every man on the place was in action. Horses were being saddled, including the golden-maned stallion of Blaise Amory. No voice among them was more militant than Amory's. "Mule thieves!" He vaulted the yard fence and raced for the barn. "Heading south? Let's after them, men. Lend me a gun, someone."

Helga dashed back upcreek, all but three of the men following asaddle. Of these three, two made a spring wagon crew and they drove away with a cot mattress spread to receive Phineas Tarber. The last man, Sam Akin, loped toward Alamosa for a doctor. Only Margie was left at the ranch. As she made the guestroom into a temporary hospital, her heart pulsed with sympathy for Helga. It might have been her own father instead of Helga's. Last summer it *had* been her own brother. Her brother Tommy who, returning from a Fourth of July celebration in Alamosa, had been met by an open pasture gate through which a dozen Wagon Wheel mounts had been driven away by thieves. Tommy McCarron and Sam Akin had given chase but only Sam had returned. Just beyond Conejos, a horse thief's bullet had knocked Tommy dead from his saddle.

Today these mule thieves were headed in the same direction. Could they be the same ones? In the past several years many horses had been driven south from the park, by stilluncaught raiders, and usually when the owners were known to be away from home. Today's raiders, Margie reasoned, could know about the Tarbers' habit of attending Sunday church at Del Norte.

She had the room ready when grinding wheels announced the return of the rescue party. Helga came in first, her fine Nordic face drawn with terror lest they were too late. Mark McCarron and Luke Priddy followed with Phineas Tarber. The cot mattress made a litter on which they brought him to the bed Margie had prepared. "He's still breathing," McCarron said.

Margie had hot water and bandages ready. But it was Helga who knew what to do with them, Helga who sent the rest of them scurrying on this errand or that. Helga who was suddenly calm and strong with steady hands as she used warm salt water as a disinfectant, and rebound the bullet-punctured body of Phineas Tarber.

Bandaged it so skillfully that Doctor Gale, when he arrived after midnight from Alamosa, praised her unreservedly. "Lucky you were along, Helga. Not a nurse this side of Denver could have done better."

He banished all but Helga from the room and they stood watch there through the night. At dawn Margie brought them coffee. "How is he?" she whispered anxiously.

"He has a bare chance," Gale told her. "But

only if he stays right where he is for at least a month."

"Of course." Margie insisted warmly. It was easy to understand that a jolting wagon ride would reopen the wound. "Come on, honey." She took Helga's hand. "I've fixed a room for you. And right now you must get some sleep."

Mark McCarron, meeting them in the hall, was no less cordial. His arm went impulsively around Helga. "This happened to my own boy a year ago. Only we got him home too late."

Sheer exhaustion made Helga sleep. When she awakened the posse of pursuing cowboys had returned. Their leader, Blaise Amory, looked grimly disgusted. "Lost their sign," he reported, "in the Conejos River right where it comes out of the canyon. No telling which way they went from there. Maybe over Cumbres and into the Chama country."

"We told the sheriff about it," Luke Priddy added, "at Conejos. You say they were forkin' bay broncs, miss?"

"They looked like bays," Helga said wearily. "But it was poor light and they were a long way off."

12

A long way off, in an opposite direction, was Tony Darrow. He sat his saddle and looked quizzically down at a stake with a rusty tin can inverted over it. The place was on Mosca Creek, at the foot of Mosca Pass, and some fifty miles northeast of the McCarron ranch. Land marks and a creek bend made the location clear to Tony. He knew he was on a certain quarter section of a certain township and range. The old toll road coming down from the pass angled across a corner of it. And directly west of him loomed one of nature's most awesome phenomena, the Great Sand Dunes of San Luis Park.

Dismounting, Tony took the can from the stake to look inside. Here, as he'd expected, was a copy of a land-filing application made a year ago. Its numbers and signature matched those on the original which had been received by mail at the Del Norte land office. At this spot an Alfred Smead had claimed for himself one hundred and sixty acres of government land, professing under oath that he wanted it for his permanent farm and home.

Yet where now was Alfred Smead? No cabin was in sight. Nor even a dugout. Not a foot of plowed land or any other sign of occupancy. All

Smead had ever done, apparently, had been the mailing of a filled-in form which he'd signed before the clerk of a county court, and the driving of this stake. His application had given General Delivery Alamosa as his address.

During recent weeks Tony had ridden all over the park and had even made an excursion over Wolf Creek Pass into the San Juan Basin. Receiver Halderman had furnished him with a list of homestead filings similar to the one made by Eusebio Sanchez. "Pussyfoot filings," Halderman was beginning to call them.

Yet in most cases Tony had found a homestead shack housing a sincere settler and his family. In seven cases he'd found what lay before him now—a blank.

He made a note of it, then rode away southward, skirting the giant dunes. They made a fantastic sight, mountains of gray sand covering sixty square miles, constantly shifting, eerily whispering, humming, even singing when wind blew stiffly from the Rio Grande. Now Tony rested his horse and sat listening to their murmurs. Close under their spell, they made him remember the legend of Luis Gonzales who in 1816 had herded three thousand sheep up here from Old Mexico. Leaving his sheep and his herders at this very spot he'd ridden alone up over Mosca Pass to explore beyond it. And returning had found a mountain of sand where his camp had been, his herders and his three thousand sheep being buried under it.

Riding on, Tony considered the homestead filing of Alfred Smead. Maybe no fraud had been intended. After filing a claim with sincerity, perhaps the man had changed his mind and quit the valley for good. In any case Halderman would now cancel the filing, restoring the quarter to the public domain.

Nightfall caught Tony at the Zapata ranch, on Medano Creek. His first question was, "Know a fella named Alfred Smead?"

"Never heard of him," the foreman said. "Light and pick your bunk, cowboy."

In six other cases it had been the same. A stake on a bare claim, and a name of which no one had ever heard.

In the morning Tony rode on south, through saddle-high sage. Twice he flushed mated sage hens and once he sighted a band of bounding antelope. The plot of a wholesale land fraud tugged at the edges of his mind but he couldn't nail it down. Could those seven names be fictitious? Had they been made up out of thin air? If not, why couldn't any of the seven men be found? There was an eighth, of course, Eusebio Sanchez. A land office acceptance of the Sanchez application had been found on the murdered body of Pancho Morales—yet no one had ever found Sanchez. The clerk of the court at Conejos had witnessed Sanchez' signature but could remember him only as a middle-aged Mexican who'd looked and smelled like a sheepherder.

Yet what good would it do to file homesteads under faked names? The same faked names would need to be signed to final proof papers three years later, and again before a clerk of a county court. In nine cases out of ten a patent deed would then be mailed from the land office to the applicant. It would be only a ghost title, Tony reasoned, because the deed would be made out to a non-existent person. And what good would land be to a ghost?

The track of the D & RG narrow gauge came in sight and Tony struck it at Fort Garland. Riding by the adobe wall of the barracks he stopped briefly at the depot. A section gang was tamping ties there. And Tony asked a question he'd already asked, weeks ago, of station agents both here and at Placer.

"Look, *amigos.* I been tryin' to locate a lawyer named Saul Spengler. He took a train outa Alamosa on a Sunday night about six weeks back. Got off either here or at Placer. Any of you happen to see him?"

Blank looks from all but one of the crew. This one asked, "Is he a *gordo*, señor?"

"That's right," Tony prompted. "He's a fatty."

"Does he have two chins with a need for shaving?"

"That's the guy. You saw him?"

"It is after dark when he gets off the last coach, señor. Another man waits here with horses. And they ride away."

"In what direction?"

The section hand pointed southwesterly, where creek brush made a green diagonal line across the great Sangre de Cristo Grant.

"Who was the guy waitin' here with horses?"

"In the dark I cannot tell, señor."

Tony went to the Fort Garland post office. "Has a man named Alfred Smead ever called for mail here?"

"Never heard of him," the postmaster said. "You from Alamosa? Say, did they ever catch those mule thieves?"

"What mule thieves?"

The man held up this week's Alamosa *Independent.* Tony, riding through the wilderness, hadn't seen it till now. A look at the headlines made him forget all about Alfred Smead.

He'd intended to follow the railroad right-of-way to Alamosa. This news story changed his mind and made him cut straight southwest down Trinchera Creek. It was the shortest route to his own homestead, and from there he could hurry on to the McCarron ranch. Phineas Tarber lay wounded and perhaps dying there. Helga was there too, and she at least would have a welcome for him. She'd seen the pair who'd shot her father and stolen the mules. Bay horses didn't mean much. The range was full of them. But maybe she could remember the sizes of the two men. If one was big and the other small, they might turn out to be Wycross and Mock.

For a month now the whereabouts of Wycross and Mock had puzzled Tony. Neither had been seen around Alamosa since the day he'd panicked them in Brophy's Bar. Diego Sandoval had stood pat, and Trigger Huggins was still around town. Only Mock and Wycross had disappeared from Brophy's.

A fair guess was they were out on the range hunting Tony from ambush, hoping to snipe from some dry arroyo as he rode by. For that reason Tony had changed his calico pony for a less conspicuous black; and he'd been careful not to tell anyone the route of his next ride. So an ambush could hardly be planned in advance.

He jogged on down the Trinchera and this was a route he'd never taken before. For it wasn't in the public domain and therefore could never be homesteaded. Everything this side of the Rio Grande and south to the New Mexico line was part of the great *merced* granted to Luis Lee and Narcisco Beaubien as a private estate in the days of Mexican sovereignty. A million-odd acres on which Tony, even now, was technically a trespasser and which he crossed only because it gave him a short cut home.

The idea came to him that if Saul Spengler,

or anyone else, wanted to hide out for a season, here would be the perfect place. Because only the *vaqueros* of the great grant rode this range, whose hub was the adobe plaza of San Luis. And those riders, a take-it-easy sort, would rarely range this far north except in the spring and fall rodeos. Even then they'd be of a temper to give any alien camper the benefit of a doubt.

This same route, Tony remembered, was the one Blaise Amory had taken on foot six years ago, on his marathon run to Fort Garland. Except that Amory had traveled in the opposite direction, up the Trinchera instead of down. Blaise Amory who, according to Unahwa the Ute, had faked the whole business to help gringo outlaws kill and rob Don Pablo Arragon.

The cold-bloodedness of it brought a revulsion to Tony. And a sense of helplessness because it couldn't be proved. Only by vague, flimsy strings could he link Amory to it, or to the murder of Morales and the disappearance of Saul Spengler.

Sight of a rock shack down the creek bottom made Tony slow to a walk. The shack was flush against a barranca which would hide it from most angles, and near it, in a rock pen, were two horses. This could be some outpost, perhaps a sheep camp, of the Sangre de Cristo Grant. But Tony proceeded with caution. The two horses could be those which, six weeks ago Sunday night, had met a train at Fort Garland.

Moving closer, Tony decided the place didn't look like it housed Mexicans. A Mexican outpost would have a dog or two, and there'd be an outdoor oven and chili peppers hanging from the eaves. To play safe, Tony rode into a creek thicket and tied his horse there. With his saddle rifle he advanced afoot down the line of willows.

When he came opposite the rock shack he saw that its door was open. No sound came from it; yet horses in the corral meant that men weren't far away. Rifle ready, Tony moved cautiously to the open door. He looked in at a dirt floor, a small table, a stove and boxes serving as chairs. A pack of frayed cards lay on the table; also an empty whisky bottle and a tall, pump-shaped metal object which Tony at first didn't recognize.

He stepped inside for a closer look. "Spengler!" he called. "Saul Spengler!" No one answered. But Spengler was surely nearby because the thing on the table was the seal of a notary public.

The place had two rooms and Tony opened a door to the rear one. Two cots were in there. Also a table with tinware where two men had eaten breakfast. One cot had only a tangle of blankets. On the other lay Spengler, fully dressed and in a sodden sleep.

Tony didn't disturb him. Instead he looked about for a motive which would make Spengler need to hide out here. He was no prisoner because the other man had left him alone in the shack.

A man who'd met him at Fort Garland with a saddled horse, and who'd doubled back here with him to a hideout which, while a bare twenty miles from Alamosa, was in another county, Costilla, and thus out of the jurisdiction of law officers both at Alamosa and Conejos.

Costilla County, consisting mainly of the great grant, was a world of its own, administered from the plaza of San Luis.

A duffel bag gave up no answers. But a drawer in the front room table had startling exhibits. A pad of U. S. Land Office homestead filing blanks. And a set of sectionized government maps showing the entire area served by the Del Norte land office.

Not a word was written on any of the blanks. Not a scrap of correspondence was anywhere about. The blanks and the maps might be for use in a bold scheme of fraudulent homestead filings—except for one kink. A notary public wasn't eligible to attest the signature of an applicant. So a crooked notary didn't fit the plot.

Yet Spengler had fled from Alamosa apparently to avoid questioning by Receiver Halderman—and co-conspirators seemed to be holding him in a convenient hideout for further service as a notary.

Footsteps on gravel alerted Tony. He put the blanks and the maps back in the drawer and swung his rifle to cover the door. In a moment a man appeared there. He was a short, blocky gringo with a square, sun-blackened face that Tony had seen often before. The man had a shotgun in one hand and two mallard ducks in the other.

He stood startled in the doorway, his slate eyes glued to Tony's rifle which, held hip-high, was pointing in his exact direction. "Where've you been, Trinidad?" Tony asked sociably.

Trinidad Jones, they called him along Front Street in Alamosa. Dangerous with a gun, they said. Tony knew him only by sight and reputation. Once the man had been night bartender at Slavick's but Slavick, who ran a reputable saloon, had soon discharged him. Tony had never seen him around Brophy's Bar.

"Duck huntin'," Trinidad said. He tossed the mallards in on the floor but kept a grip on his shotgun. Its angle wasn't quite right for a quick blast at Tony Darrow.

"What's Spengler doin' here?" Tony's head jerked toward the back room.

"Rest cure." The response was glib and could have been prepared for just such an encounter. "He got delirium tremens so I fetched him to the country. Simple life here's makin' a new man outa him."

A click behind Tony could be the cocking of a gun. Or the turning of a doorknob. A flick of Trinidad's eyes in that direction and a new composure on his face warned Tony that Saul Spengler was awake and peering in here. He might have a gun in his hand. If so, Tony was between two fires and didn't have a chance.

When Trinidad Jones spoke again his voice had confidence and his eyes a threat. "What are *you* doin' here, mister?"

"Waitin' for Sheriff Billy Carson," Tony answered carelessly. "Seen anything of him? He said for me to meet him here."

"I ain't seen him. And I don't think you have either." Nevertheless some of the composure faded from Trinidad's face. He stepped outside for a quick glance southeast, in which direction lay San Luis, the county seat. For this was Costilla County and its sheriff just happened to be the son of a world-famous scout named Kit Carson.

It was a name to conjure with and Tony conjured with it now. "It's time I'm movin' on. Mind passin' a message to Billy when he comes?"

Blocking the doorway with his shotgun, the slanting slate eyes of Trinidad Jones were half jeering and half fearful. "What message?"

"Tell him Jess Fritchie'll have the prisoner here by sundown."

"What prisoner?"

"Fella named Lew Wager. Don't you guys read the papers?" Tony sauntered toward the exit where Trinidad stood with his shotgun. Spengler, if armed, could shoot him in the back. But would he dare, after mention of Carson and Fritchie?

Fritchie, the sheriff of Conejos County and Carson, sheriff of Costilla. The Rio Grande was the county line; so if Lew Wager's felony had been in Costilla County and he'd been captured in Conejos, courtesy would require Fritchie to turn the man over to Carson. And this rock cabin would make a convenient meeting place for the delivery.

Ten to one it wasn't true, but one to ten it was.

The bare possibility leashed the triggers of Saul Spengler and Trinidad Jones. Killing Tony just before the arrival of two sheriffs was a thing to make them think twice. As far as Tony knew, neither Carson nor Fritchie was looking for Wager. Yet Lew Wager had been publicized as a criminal, so the illusion wasn't illogical.

Before Trinidad Jones could decide whether he was being sold a bill of goods, Tony had shouldered by him and was outside the cabin. He turned to keep his rifle aimed at Trinidad's stomach.

"That duck gun makes me nervous, Trinidad. Drop it." Tony, no longer between two fires, thumbed back the rifle's hammer. The shotgun clattered to the threshold.

Beyond, peering from the back room, stood Saul Spengler. A disheveled Spengler with bloodshot eyes, his face hairy and bloated.

"You'd better drop yours too," Tony suggested. As he swung his aim to Spengler a revolver fell from the man's hand.

"Both of you come on out and we'll take a walk."

The notary came cringing from the cabin and Tony marched the two upcreek to his horse. There was no use, he decided, making any charges against them. They had as much right to be here as he had himself. It was no crime to buy a ticket to Pueblo and get off the train at Fort Garland. Nor was it a crime to own a pad of blank forms.

Nothing of importance could be proved on Saul Spengler, least of all that he was being used illegally by Blaise Amory.

Tony led his horse from the willows and mounted. "Keep outa trouble, you guys." He waved a hand at the two men and loped down-creek toward the Rio Grande.

13

Crossing it at the mouth of the Trinchera put Tony in Conejos County. A mile below the Conejos came in from the other side and Tony, riding up the Conejos, arrived presently at the ruins of Zebulon Pike's stockade.

The historic antiquity of it awed him a little. For it was here that Captain Zebulon Pike, on an exploration in the year 1807, had built a fort of mud bricks and logs and had unfurled the American flag over it. He'd supposed he was still in the new Louisiana Purchase and learned better only when one Juan Bautista de Anza appeared with a troop of Spanish soldiers. "You trespass, señor," de Anza had announced. "For this is land of the King of Spain who has made me the governor of Sonora and of all the great Southwest." After credentials and maps had proved this to be true, Zebulon Pike had struck his colors and submitted to arrest.

It was nearly dark when Tony passed the place and two miles on up the Conejos he came to his own homestead. "Pour yourself some java," Chuck Gleason greeted. But Tony, staring at the starlit outline of cabin, barely heard him. Everything seemed to be done except the top half of a chimney and shingles for the lean-to.

Tony took a lantern and made a tour of inspection. "You're a wizard," he said gratefully to Bill Epps.

Chuck assumed a hurt look. "What about *me?* It was me coaxed the whole Jaybird crew over here on Sundays, to lend a hand."

Epps added with a grin: "But they didn't tell Blaise Amory about it. Next time you come by you can move right in."

"Where you headed now, Tony?"

"The McCarron place," Tony said. "To see if the Tarbers are still there."

"They'll likely be there a month yet," Chuck guessed. "Blaise Amory spends half his time there, shinin' around Margie. He's the fair-haired boy, that fella. Seems like nobody's mad at him 'cept you and me."

"Us and a Ute Indian," Tony amended.

The McCarrons had just finished breakfast when Tony knocked at their door. Margie opened it and the beginning of a smile died on her face. Tony remembered her last bitter words: "Please don't ever speak to me again, Tony Darrow."

But now her voice, while not friendly, had no rancor. "Hello. You want to see Helga, I suppose."

"And you too, Margie. I've been wanting to see you a long time." Tony stood twisting his hat, waiting for her to ask him in. Then Mark McCarron loomed back of her in the hall. "Show him into the parlor, Margie." The man's voice had no warmth in it. "Then leave him to me."

Margie led the way to a parlor. "I'll call Helga, Tony." She said it without even looking at him, and disappeared.

Mark McCarron took a spread-legged stance in front of Tony. "Get this straight," he said. "Blaise Amory's my friend and neighbor. I expect him to be a member of my family some day. So if you've any charges against him don't make them to my ears. Or on my property. Understand?"

"I didn't come here to talk about Amory." Tony's face was afire but he fought down an impulse to lash back at McCarron. "I just want to see Mr. Tarber. . . ."

"You can't see him," the rancher cut in. "Doctor's orders."

"I'm afraid that's right, Tony." It was Helga speaking from the doorway. "Doctor Gale says no visitors." She smiled and it made her beautiful. "But it's awfully nice of you to ask."

Doctor Gale had brought her a nurse's white dress and Tony thought she looked lovely in it. McCarron said stiffly, "Make yourself at home, Darrow," and left the room.

Tony laughed uncomfortably. "He doesn't like me."

"Sit down, Tony," Helga said. "Can you blame him? Blaise is like a son to him and you've said such terrible things!"

“Let’s forget Amory,” Tony said irritably. “How’s your father getting along?”

Helga brightened. “He’s over the crisis. Right now he’s sleeping and in no pain. But he can’t be moved for a long time yet.”

“Then maybe you could take a couple of hours off,” Tony suggested hopefully.

“I could. Margie would be glad to sit by his bed. But why?”

“I read the news story about your chase after mule rustlers. It said they stopped to feed their broncs and boil coffee as they crossed Gato Creek.”

“That’s right, they did.”

“Could you show me the place?”

Helga hadn’t been asaddle for days and the prospect pleased her. “If it would help to catch those two men,” she said quickly.

“There’s a chance it will.”

“Wait till I change. It won’t take but a minute.”

He waited in the parlor and it took more than a minute. He hoped Margie would come in but she didn’t. Tony picked up a copy of the *Rocky Mountain News* and glanced through it. A fine new hotel called the Windsor, it said, was being opened in Denver.

Helga came in dressed as when she’d fought off wolves on a snowbound trail. It was the man’s outfit she’d worn on the chase after mule thieves with her father. "Margie will take care of him till noon," she said.

They went to the barn and saddled her horse. Soon they were riding up Alamosa Creek toward the route of the chase. Reaching it they turned north toward Gato Creek. "What," Helga asked, "do you hope to find there?"

"I don't know," Tony brooded. "But they were there long enough to make coffee and grain their horses. Once an old-timer said to me: 'A man leaves something at every camp he makes, all through life.' "

"At a long camp," Helga agreed. "But hardly at a short one."

"Even at a short one," Tony argued, "he could smoke a cigaret. Coffee and a cigaret—they go together. If he smokes a cigaret he flips away the butt. A brown paper butt, maybe."

When she looked sidewise at him he explained: "Pinky Mock smokes brown paper cigarets. He and a man named Wycross left Alamosa a month ago and haven't been seen there since. They're toughies who don't work for an honest living. I think they're in on a big land grab—but maybe they steal horses on the side. One's big and one's little."

"One of the two I saw seemed bigger than the other," Helga remembered. "But they were a long way off in the twilight and I can't be sure."

They came to Gato Creek and rode into a

copse of scrub aspen. "This is the place." Helga dismounted by the ashes of an old fire. The oat grains dropped from the mouths of feeding horses had been cleaned up by birds and chipmunks. But a can with old coffee grounds was still there.

Tony cut two forked sticks and gave one to the girl. A boulder lay to one side of the ashes and a log on the other. "With coffee and a cigaret," Tony guessed, "one guy would sit on the rock and the other on the log. Let's rake around for a brown paper snipe."

Helga wasn't hopeful. "Lots of men use brown paper for cigarets."

"Sure. So if we find a *white* paper butt we'll know the guy wasn't Mock." Tony raked dust and leaves by the boulder. Helga did the same by the log.

Neither of them found anything discarded by a smoker. Not even a burned match. Tony widened his circle of search and finally gave up. "It was a bum hunch," he admitted.

"Here's something, Tony." An object bright and metallic among the leaves had caught Helga's eye. She picked it up and Tony saw that it was a small, flat key.

"Looks like a padlock key," he concluded.

"You think one of them dropped it?"

"Somebody did. And not too long ago because it hasn't started to rust." Since the mule thieves were the last people to camp here, it was more than probable that one of them had dropped the key. "He could fish it outa his pocket with a match, without knowing it."

With this single find they rode back to the Wagon Wheel ranch. Tony opened the ranch gate for Helga but didn't go in himself. "Better I stop right here," he grinned. "I've been poison to 'em ever since I tangled with Blaise Amory."

Her clear blue eyes searched him as she held her horse in the open gate. "You're keeping something back, aren't you? Something about a Ute Indian?"

He remembered his cryptic answer to a news editor. "Find a Ute Indian named Unahwa. . . ." Helga and the McCarrons and the entire park would have read that interview in the *Independent*'s next issue.

"I'll let you in on it if you'll keep it to yourself," Tony said with an abrupt decision.

"I won't tell," Helga promised.

"You know about the old Arragon massacre. It happened right where I'm building my cabin. Not long ago I found an Indian chopping into a log . . ." Tony gave her Unahwa's sensational charge against Blaise Amory.

"Oh no! He couldn't!" Helga protested. But she knew that Utes were riflemen and not pistol packers. As a child she and her father had themselves been besieged by Utes in the cabin above Del Norte. "Would you take the word of a strange Indian . . . against Blaise Amory's?"

Her quick defense of the man angered Tony. "You would too," he flung back, "if he'd tried to kill you with that stallion of his. And some day I'll prove it on him."

"How?" Her level gaze challenged him.

He took a padlock key from his pocket and gazed at it grimly. "Look, Helga. You could help me a lot."

She glanced over her shoulder toward the ranch house. "I've been gone too long," she worried. "I must get back to father."

"Just a minute, please," he begged, and rode close to her. "Chuck says Amory comes callin' here every Sunday. This is Saturday so he ought to be here tomorrow."

She nodded, her eyes puzzled. "He's invited to noon dinner tomorrow."

"At the table," Tony suggested, "suppose you tell about our finding a padlock key dropped by the mule thieves. And see what happens."

As she stared blankly he went on: "Just say we found the key and I put it in my pocket. Which is the truth. Then say I figure the rustlers dropped it. And so I aim to find a padlock somewhere that fits the key. Maybe on a barn door or a pasture gate; or on a door in town or maybe on some shanty door in a canyon hideout. Just tell it at the Sunday dinner table, in front of Amory, and see what happens."

"Nothing," Helga scoffed, "could possibly happen."

"I'll make a bet with you," Tony offered grimly. "Amory won't stay all afternoon, makin' pretty talk to Margie like he usually does. Right after dinner he'll rig up some excuse and ride away."

Helga smiled. "You're just imagining all this, Tony," she chided. "What on earth could Blaise Amory have to do with the mule thieves? But just to prove you're wrong I'll do it. I'll tell about the key at dinner tomorrow." Wheeling her horse she galloped to the house.

Shortly after noon on Sunday, Tony and Chuck staked out in a scrub oak thicket which overlooked the McCarron ranch. The house was half a mile away but they'd been able to make out Blaise Amory on his sorrel stallion, a few minutes ago, as he'd arrived for dinner. "He unsaddled and turned the brute in the corral," Chuck muttered, "so he figures to stay all afternoon."

"If he does I'll lose a bet." Today Tony was pessimistic. A lost padlock key might not concern Amory at all. Any crime of Mock and Wycross should concern him, but there was still no solid reason to believe that Mock and Wycross had stolen the mules.

"We'll soon know, *amigo*." Chuck settled down to wait patiently.

"We *do* know!" Tony exulted less than an hour

later. For he saw Amory emerge and hurry to the corral. There the man saddled his stallion and rode away.

"Didn't even take time to pick his teeth," Gleason chuckled. "And look! He's headin' south. Same way the mules went."

The Jaybird ranch lay east of the Wagon Wheel. So the man's southerly course meant he wasn't going home. "The way he's headin'," Chuck concluded, "he'll wind up in Conejos."

They let him get almost out of sight before following. This wasn't difficult because Amory made no effort to keep under cover. Instead he rode openly along a wagon trail leading to the county seat.

He crossed the upper La Jara and went on past Diamond Springs. Tony and Chuck kept a cautious half mile behind. In two hours Amory made fifteen miles and rode into the sleepy plaza of Conejos.

A one-story adobe courthouse had *tiendas* facing it from three sides. No one was in sight at this siesta hour. A stranger wouldn't believe that this could be the seat of a county bigger in area than New Jersey.

Tall hollyhocks swayed in the afternoon heat. A mud church made one side of the plaza and along the Conejos River, which Amory had to ford before entering town, giant cottonwoods gave coolness and shade. Here Tony and Chuck closed in a little. They were in time to see Amory ride through the plaza without stopping.

A mile beyond it he drew up at a shabby adobe house by the trail. Amory dismounted and was admitted there. In a few minutes he came out and stepped back into his saddle. From a screen of cottonwoods Tony saw him ride directly back along the route over which he'd come.

They kept under cover as he passed them. "Don't I smell goats, Chuck?"

"You sure do, Tony. Leo Cimino lives in that shack. He's got a herd o' goats and he makes goat cheese. There he is now." A wiry, sharp-featured Italian came out and hurried to a shed. There he saddled a horse and tied a blanket roll back of the saddle.

"Amory," Tony guessed shrewdly, "sent him on a ride."

"Shall we follow Amory back home?"

"No, Chuck. Let's follow Leo Cimino."

14

Leo Cimino jogged south toward the state line. Presently he crossed the new narrow-gauge track, which had missed Conejos due to right-of-way troubles. Beyond the track the trail forked, one fork turning up the mountain canyon of the Conejos River while the other continued on down the main valley of the Rio Grande. Cimino took the latter fork, Tony and Chuck keeping well out of his sight.

"Nothing better than goats," Chuck observed, "to cover up horse tracks. Say these fellas steal broncs and drive 'em south to about here. They make a fake trail up the Conejos Canyon a little piece, then cross the river and double back. But Cimino drives goats along this back-lap and so nobody ever sees it."

"They could work it over and over," Tony agreed. "Get ready for a gunfight, Chuck. Chances are Cimino's on his way to ditch a padlock. He might lead us bang into a shack fulla horse thieves. I'd sure like to pick up those mules and take 'em back to the Tarbers."

Ahead, Leo Cimino rode openly along a trail which in the main followed San Antonio Creek and which by nightfall brought them to the New Mexico line. Shortly beyond this the man stopped to make a creek-bank camp.

"Up to us to do the same," Chuck said. They picked a brushy spot well downcreek from Cimino and offsaddled. Chuck had coffee and bacon in his blanket roll.

The morning sun was an hour high before the little goatman broke camp. He continued on south and the cowboys kept him in sight. To the right were volcanic mountains and to the left the valley of the Rio Grande. "He's hittin' for Taos," Chuck guessed. But midmorning proved him wrong as the man ahead veered westerly on a side trail. San Antonio and Ortiz Peaks lay that way, and the lava-pitted Rio Arriba country whose trading center was Tierra Amarilla.

Scrub oak canyons slashed deep into San Antonio Peak and Cimino rode directly toward one of them. Brush permitted the trailers to close in a little. And soon they saw a pole fence spanning the narrow entrance of a box canyon. The fence had a high frame gate at which Cimino dismounted.

Tony and Chuck watched him from a thicket no more than a furlong away. The gate had a chain and padlock. They saw Cimino take a key from his pocket and unlock the padlock. They supposed he'd open the gate and go in. But he didn't. A small creeklet trickled out of the canyon. Leo Cimino tossed the padlock into the creek. He stood for a moment looking idly into the water and rolling a cigaret. Then he climbed stiffly to his saddle and rode back over the route on which he'd come.

"Shall we grab him?" Chuck whispered.

"Let him go," Tony said.

When the goatman had passed them and was well out of sight, Tony rode to the creeklet and fished out the padlock. He tried his key in it. "It fits, Chuck."

"Well, whadda yuh know!" Chuck grinned. "All we got to do now is go tip the sheriff at Conejos."

But Tony knew it wasn't that simple. "Tip him to what, Chuck? That Cimino threw away a padlock? No law against that. No law against Blaise Amory stopping by to see a goatman; he'd say he just stopped there to order a load of cheese."

"Let's see what's on the other side of this fence," Chuck insisted.

They opened the gate and passed through. The canyon was narrow, straight, sheer-walled and fed by a tiny stream.

Shortly it pinched to a bottleneck and across this was a second fence with a gate. This gate was wire and had no lock.

Beyond it the canyon opened out again but at no place was it more than a quarter mile wide. Its grassy floor would make good pasture and Tony saw horse sign. No stock was now in sight. "Them mules've come and gone," Chuck muttered.

"Look out, Chuck!" Tony reined to a stop, snatching a carbine from his saddle boot. A couple of cabins loomed ahead. Directly beyond them the canyon came to a steep blind end.

Chuck stepped to the ground with a drawn forty-five. "Keep close to the crik and they won't see us." He led his horse into creek-bank brush and Tony followed him there. "Might be no one's at home," Tony said. "You see any chimney smoke?"

"Never mind chimney smoke, *amigo.* Just watch out for gunsmoke. That there's too big a layout not to have any hands around."

They tied their mounts and moved quietly up the screen of brush. It took them to a corral which, although droppings proved recent use, was now empty. Nor did either of the two cabins show any life. "Guess we don't get to throw any lead after all," Gleason's tone sounded disappointed.

"Been no cattle here," Tony concluded after an inspection of the corral. "Nothing but horses."

"And mules," Chuck corrected. He pointed to a shod print too small and narrow for a horse.

Tony punched his rifle out in front of him and advanced to a cabin door. "Cover me, Chuck." A knock brought no response. Tony kicked the door open and what he saw inside made him turn to Chuck with a sheepish grin. "We sure walked into it. Lucky they aren't at home!"

"They'd a sure burned us down," Chuck agreed. The cabin had bunks and blankets for ten men. "And they ain't been gone long, either. Here's a Taos paper only three days old."

They went to the other cabin and found a cooking setup. A stock of canned food and a table for ten boarders. Tony whistled. "They come and go, Chuck. See if you can find anything that'll tie 'em to Amory."

A search produced nothing but a small metal disc. It was a beer check issued by Brophy's Bar in Alamosa.

"What'll we do?" Chuck brooded. "Hightail for home? Or wait for 'em to come back and trade 'em a few bullets?"

"Neither," Tony decided. "Let's ride to the nearest neighbor and ask him who owns this canyon."

"One thing's a cinch," Chuck concluded. "Only one way in or out of this deadfall and that's through the padlocked gate."

They rode back to it and out of the canyon. "Wonder why Cimino didn't put a new lock on the gate when he tossed the old one away."

"They'll put on a new lock," Tony surmised, "after they've had time to have duplicate keys made. A ten-man gang'd need ten keys."

Chuck Gleason had once ridden roundup down this way and knew a cowman named Clardy in the foothills about five miles east. “Honest as daylight,” Chuck said as they headed that way.

“George Chester owns that canyon,” Clardy told them. “He proved up on it ’bout two year ago.”

“It’s only a quarter section?” Tony asked.

“Yep, one of those long quarters. A mile long by a quarter mile wide. Just the right shape to cover that box canyon. I figgered to buy it, last summer, ’cause I need another water-hole over that way. So I rode over to Tierra Amarilla to look up the title.”

“And found George Chester owns it?”

“That’s right. The government issued him a patent to it and since then he’s mailed in his taxes every spring to the county treasurer. But dagged if I’ve ever been able to find him.”

“You mean he doesn’t live on the place?”

Clardy cupped a match to light his pipe. “Nope. Nobody seems to live there. And I can’t find anyone who even knows this fella Chester. If you run on to him, tell him I’ll give him a top price for that canyon.”

Tony and Chuck rode away. “We sure will, Mr. Clardy.”

At the main trail they turned north toward Colorado. “Know what I think, Chuck? It’s a turn-over station for stolen horses.”

“Could be,” Chuck muttered. “Two gangs. One

steals broncs in Colorado. The other sells 'em in New Mex and Texas."

"The Colorado gang," Tony guessed, "makes a fast drive to that padlocked canyon. They leave the horses there and hit for home. If a posse tracks the horses there, they don't find any men. If they look up a land title they find the name George Chester. But Chester's only a ghost, so they can't arrest him."

Chuck cocked an eye. "A ghost, you say?"

"Maybe not. But I've found eight homesteads up in Conejos and Saguache counties filed by names nobody's ever seen in the flesh. This could be another one—a claim filed under a phoney name and proved up by mail."

Chuck whistled softly. "So they leave the broncs there till rain and wind and goats spoil tracks. Then the sellin' crew comes up from New Mex and drives 'em on south."

"They could even forge the name George Chester to a bill of sale," Tony said. "It would be something to show if a sheriff stopped 'em. The law couldn't do a thing but start looking for George Chester."

Hours after dark they rode into Conejos and put up at the little hotel there. And when Tony awoke in the morning his bedmate was gone. It had been agreed that Chuck should hurry on to help Bill Epps.

After breakfast Tony wrote and mailed a letter

to Receiver Halderman at Del Norte. It ended: "So if you can spare the time to come down here, it might pay us to look up a few titles."

Since the letter must go by stage, Halderman couldn't be expected for several days. Tony filled the time by riding up Conejos Canyon all the way to its head, where there was a mining settlement called Conejos Camp. The round trip of a hundred miles took two days going up and two coming back down.

En route Tony checked nine filings on the list given him by Halderman. On six he found bona fide settlers. On three he found nothing; nor anyone who'd seen or heard of the claimants.

On the fifth day Tony rode back into Conejos Plaza. Halderman wasn't at the hotel. But at the post office was a letter announcing he'd arrive a day later. Tony, absorbed in reading it as he left the post office, bumped into someone who was coming in.

He stood back, confused, and pulled off his hat. "Margie!"

"Hello, Tony." Her voice and eyes had the old gay friendliness—but only for a moment. "I was about to mail a letter." This in a tone which again shut him out of her life. A stamped letter was in her hand. She went by him and into the post office.

It wasn't strange that she'd be here, Conejos being nearly as close to the Wagon Wheel as

Alamosa. Much of the Wagon Wheel shopping was done here. Margie mailed her letter and came out again. A straw leghorn hat covered her red curls and Tony knew by her dress that she hadn't come horseback. He was eager to get back on the old footing. As she crossed the plaza he fell in step beside her. "Is Mr. Tarber still at your place, Margie?"

"Yes." The wide brim of her hat kept him from seeing her face. She went on toward a Wagon Wheel rig tied in front of Garcia's store.

"Is he getting along all right?"

"Why don't you ask Helga? There she is."

Helga Tarber came out of Garcia's with her arms full of bundles. They met her at the rig. "Tony!" She was surprised and frankly pleased to see him. How natural and genuine she was! Tony thought. "Where have you been, Tony?" she asked.

"Winning a bet," he said, remembering his last parting with her. A gleam in her eyes meant she understood, and conceded he *had* won it. For Blaise Amory *had* made an abruptly premature departure last Sunday. Margie, watching them, looked confused. Tony covered up by asking what the girls were doing in Conejos.

"Costumes," Helga laughed, "for the Fourth of July *baile*." There was to be a fancy ball at the Perry House on the Fourth, just as there'd been last year. "We're going as señoritas," Helga announced, “so we must shop for Spanish shawls and fans and high combs.”

“You came to the right place.” Tony grinned. The atmosphere at Conejos was strictly Mexican, while Alamosa was pure raw gringo.

A man crossing toward the courthouse caught his eye. He was a blocky man, scraggly bearded, wearing chaps and a gun, and with coarse black hair showing under his hat brim. Something about his build and gait seemed vaguely familiar to Tony. As he tried to place the man Margie said briskly: “We’ve a lot to do yet and it’s getting late. Come on, Helga.”

“It was nice seeing you, Tony.” Helga smiled and let Margie lead her to a millinery shop up the walk.

Tony crossed to the courthouse in the wake of the man who’d just gone in there. *Where have I seen that fella?* He stepped into a cool, adobe corridor where the walls were two bricks thick. A sign on a door said: CLERK OF THE COUNTY COURT.

The door was open and a man was signing a paper at a counter. A county officer with a round brown face was laconically administering an oath. The signer held up his right hand. He was the man with the scraggly black beard and buckskin chaps.

As he emerged Tony stepped out of sight in the next doorway. A moment later Tony went into the court clerk's office. "Who was that fella?"

"He is Nathan Kettleman," the clerk said, "from Pagosa Springs. He is filing a homestead on the La Manga."

"You know him personally?"

The clerk shrugged. "But of course not, señor. How can I know everyone in a county so big as Conejos?"

"Thanks." Tony hurried outside. Nathan Kettleman wasn't in sight but it wasn't hard to guess where he'd gone. Crossing to the post office Tony was in time to see the man address an envelope at the public counter.

Nathan Kettleman then produced sixteen dollars—three fives and a one—and clipped it to a homestead application which he'd just signed before a proper authority. He put it all in the envelope, sealed it and dropped it into a mail slot.

Tony was waiting on the sidewalk as the man came out. "You're Kettleman?" he challenged.

The man whirled, backed off a pace. His hand brushed the butt of his gun. "Yeh, Kettleman's my name. What of it?"

Recognition flashed—for Tony knew him by his voice. "Here on a little errand for Blaise Amory, are you? Sheriff's office is right across the plaza. Let's amble over there and have a talk with him."

The man's hand moved faster than Tony's eye and Tony felt the bullet before his own gun was half out. He went down with a roaring in his ears and his head felt as though a pile driver had dropped there. His chin bumped the walk and groggily he heard the man running for his horse. Then with a mighty effort Tony came up on all fours and finally to his knees. He got his gun out and began shooting. *I've got to stop him . . . can't let him get away. . . .*

His head was pounding and blood ran hot through his hair. His first shot was wide. His second plowed dust between the man's feet and made him whirl about. The man fired three times at Tony and glass crashed from the post office window. Four doors down the walk two ranch girls stood by a Wagon Wheel rig, staring in wild terror as Tony shot it out with Nathan Kettleman.

With his last shell Tony dropped the man and saw him double up in the plaza dust. Then Tony himself gave way to dizziness. He went facedown on the board walk and for minutes failed to hear even the noisy crowd which assembled about him.

He came out of it to feel a soft hand on his cheek and a tender voice call his name. "Tony!" He became aware that his head was pillowed on a girl's lap and he assumed she was Helga Tarber. "Tony!" she whispered. "They're bringing a doctor and you're going to be all right." Her voice was like a caress.

He opened his eyes and saw she wasn't Helga, but Margie. The shock of it made him sit bolt upright. His hand went to his throbbing head and touched a cloth someone had wrapped there. Then Helga pushed through the crowd with a doctor.

A quick look told the doctor that Tony's wound was superficial. A bullet had plowed along his scalp with the effect of a hammer blow, but the groove was only skin deep. Tony smiled sheepishly. He scrambled up and helped Margie to her feet.

"Lota fuss over nothin'," he mumbled.

County Sheriff Jess Fritchie appeared looking rather grim. "You killed that man, Darrow," he announced brusquely.

For a moment Tony ignored him. "Thanks, Helga. Sorry I let you in for this, Margie." Then he turned to Fritchie. "Let's have a look at him. Come on, sheriff."

He walked down the street a little way with Fritchie at his heels. A knot of citizens hovered about a dead man there. "Go ask the clerk of the court," Tony said. "He'll tell you this man just filed a homestead, under oath, as Nathan Kettleman."

Leaning over the dead man, Tony grasped a scraggly beard and a thatch of coarse black hair. When he straightened he brought the beard and hair up with him. It left the dead man with a clean-shaven chin and a nearly bald head. "Know him, sheriff?"

Jess Fritchie gaped. "Sure I know him. He's Trinidad Jones of Alamosa."

15

Tony rested that night at the Conejos hotel and every tongue on the plaza paid him tribute. For exposure of Trinidad Jones as one who'd attempted to steal land from the public domain was like exposing him at the robbing of a bank. The sheriff was mad, and so was all of Conejos. "No wonder he cut loose on you!" Fritchie slapped Tony on the back. "And you sure did a good job bringin' him down."

Coroner Celestino Romero stopped by. "In my book, señor," he said in his soft, polite voice, "I am writing that deceased met death while he flees from a felony. The County of Conejos thanks you, señor."

A livery team arrived from the north and Guy Halderman got out of it. He went in and registered for a room. Tony stood by and at a cautious nod from Halderman he followed the receiver upstairs.

Behind a locked door Tony told him everything he knew or suspected about Blaise Amory. "I figure he's back of both deals, Mr. Halderman. Land grabbing and horse grabbing."

The small gray man from Del Norte looked thoughtfully into space, pursing his lips. "What does the sheriff think?"

“I haven’t told him yet. All he knows is that Trinidad Jones filed a claim under a phoney name and began throwing lead when I jumped him about it. No reason for him to think Amory’s tied in.”

“Maybe he’s not,” Halderman brooded. “So let’s keep his name out of it till something breaks.”

Tony stared. “What more of a break do we want?”

The receiver gave a sad smile and shook his head. “It still leaves Amory a mile in the clear. Add up what you’ve got. You saw Pancho Morales knock at his door. Later you saw an alcoholic notary knock at the same door. Both of them had a right to. Later Amory tried to kill you with his horse, but it’s only your word against his. Twice he flipped away a cigaret and each time a triggerman picked it up. For that we have the word of a kicked-out bum who’s left the country. Later Amory rode fifteen miles for a word with a goatman named Cimino. But we can’t prove what he said to Cimino.”

Tony rolled a cigaret restlessly. Halderman was right. Charging a connection between Amory and Trinidad Jones would only put the Jaybird man on guard.

“We must flush him into the open,” Halderman insisted. “Any ideas?”

“I could make a guess or two,” Tony offered.

"Go ahead."

"Guess number one: after the Arragon massacre in '74 Amory met the killers for a divvy. Guess number two: a year or so later they figured out a horse rustling racket. Filed a blind canyon for a turn-over station, using the fake name of George Chester. Half the gang drove horses to it; the other half drove them on to markets. Guess number three; in three years, sending all papers by mail, they got a patent title in George Chester's name. Guess number four: this worked out so easy they decided to try it wholesale, using a flock of names and disguises, all over the San Luis Valley."

Halderman made a string of "A's" across the paper in front of him. "Up till now they could get away with it," he admitted, "nine times out of ten. Because we've only been able to check in the field on about one application in ten. But even in the tenth case they'd run no risk of being caught; because if a check showed the land unoccupied, we'd do nothing but cancel that one filing."

"What I can't dope out," Tony puzzled, "is what they want with a crooked notary! You said land papers can't be signed before a notary."

"That's right," Halderman said. "But once the land office mails a patent title to a filer at some general delivery address, the gang could then forge the same fictitious name to a warranty deed.

A deed made out to, for instance, Blaise Amory. Amory could boldly put the deed on record at the courthouse; if questioned later he'd say it was a routine land speculation such as he makes from time to time. And the law couldn't touch him with a ten-foot pole."

"What about the eleven unproved filings I've found so far—where there's nothing but a stake in the sand?"

"Those I'll revoke at once." Halderman took a list of names from his pocket. "These meet the conditions you mentioned in your letter. Let's check them at the courthouse."

They went out and crossed the plaza. "How many?" Tony asked.

"Nineteen. And if your hunch is right, Tony, they sure made a sucker out of Uncle Sam."

The county recorder made them welcome and put a stack of record books in front of them. "If I can be of further service, call me, gentlemen." He retired, leaving them alone.

"These nineteen listed homesteads," Halderman reviewed, "all meet five peculiar conditions. Title has been issued by the land office. The patentees never appeared in person at the land office and they gave only a general delivery address. In each case the filing fee was pinned in currency to the application. And last, in none of the nineteen cases was any inspection ever made on the ground."

He took the first name: Luther Young, General Delivery, Pagosa Springs, Colorado. The land involved lay on the San Juan River, a three-day ride to the west, and patent had been issued in August, 1879. Halderman opened the county book to the month of September, 1879 and found that Luther Young had put his title properly on record.

"Probably did it by mail," the receiver murmured. Then, leafing a page or two further on, he got a jolt. "Look, Tony! Here's another entry for that same quarter section. In October of '79 Luther Young sold it for 'one dollar and other consideration.' Sold it to *George Chester!*"

Tony looked at the record. The deed to George Chester had been notarized by Saul Spengler. Which at once explained Spengler. For any notary public could attest a warranty deed.

Eighteen other patents were checked with exactly the same result. In each case the patentee had a month later sold his land to George Chester, the deed in each case being notarized by Spengler.

Tony whacked a fist into palm. "And Chester, I'll bet, signed over the whole caboodle to Blaise Amory!"

Of this, however, there was no record. A painstaking search failed to turn up Amory's name in connection with any land filing.

"But someone must have paid taxes on these

nineteen quarters," Halderman exclaimed. "Let's go see the county treasurer."

Across the hall the county treasurer remembered the name. "George Chester? But of course, gentlemen. He owns three thousand acres of choice land. It is in many separate parcels but I put his taxes all on one bill. And this he has paid promptly."

"He sent you a check?" Halderman suggested hopefully.

"No," the treasurer remembered with a smile. "Chester's attorney called in person and paid the taxes in cash. An Alamosa attorney, I believe, named Spengler."

Tony and Halderman exchanged baffled looks. To plan a next move they went out to a bench under the plaza cottonwoods. "Best we don't mention Amory's name, or even George Chester's," Halderman decided, "until we pick up Saul Spengler."

"They're holding that guy under cover," Tony reminded him.

"Likely they've changed his hideout," Halderman reasoned, "after you flushed him in the Trinchera Creek cabin. He's our key witness, all right, and maybe the only one we can crack open. You say he's an old soak? Then maybe he'd sing his head off for a jug of liquor."

"Keep it away from him for a day or two," Tony nodded, "and I'd bet on it. Meantime I got an idea for knocking off everybody except Amory and Spengler."

"How?"

"Every honest outfit in the park'll be in Alamosa for the big Fourth of July celebration. They'll fan broncs all day and dance all night. The George Chester gang always picks times like that to drive horses south."

"You think it'll happen again?"

"Why not? They'll be one man short—Trinidad Jones. That's all."

Halderman mulled it over. What had happened to Trinidad Jones would be in the papers, of course; and it would scare the gang away from any further land filings. But probably from nothing else. It would seem they could carry on as usual with the business of stealing horses.

"Chuck and I and a coupla sheriffs," Tony proposed eagerly, "can be waiting at the padlocked gate."

The Fourth dawned warm and clear in Alamosa. For two days the population of the park had been pouring into town. Entire families in holiday spirit came trekking in—ahorseback and in wagons. The town as yet had no fairgrounds, but a strip along the river had been equipped with bronco chutes, corrals, race track, lemonade stands and striped awnings to shield feminine complexions from the sun. There the crowd assembled early, hawkers passing among them to vend popcorn and multi-colored balloons.

Mark McCarron had brought Margie and Helga in the evening before and the girls had a room at the Perry House. Helga had protested against staying away from her father so long, but Phineas himself had insisted on it. He was out of danger now and a capable Mexican housekeeper was there to look after him. There'd been very little fun in Helga's life, on the rugged Tarber homestead, and Phineas didn't want her to miss a chance now.

Ed Murdy, the Jaybird foreman, was squiring her today. The two girls sat on camp stools under an awning and watched as an outlaw horse was released from a chute. Ed Murdy was up, and he made a good ride of it. He sat tall and loose in the saddle, an iron-muscled man with sandy hair. This made the third occasion on which he'd paid special attention to Helga and she frankly liked him. She knew he was unequivocably honest and that his life was an open book. Even Tony Darrow and Chuck Gleason admitted that much. All of which tended to dissipate any half-formed suspicion against Blaise Amory. Tony, Helga decided, had let personal bitterness warp his judgment of Blaise. For Ed Murdy was Blaise's foreman and surely Ed wouldn't work for a dishonest employer.

Both girls clapped lustily as Murdy finished his

ride. “He’s waving his hat at you, Helga,” Margie teased.

“I hope he dances,” Helga laughed, “as well as he rides.” Yet even as she said it her eyes searched the crowd for Tony Darrow.

Tony lay in ambush with a seven-man posse sixty miles to the south. Brush hid them from whoever might enter a gate at the mouth of a narrow box canyon. Since this was Rio Arriba County, New Mexico, four of the posse were deputies from Tierra Amarilla. The others were Tony, Chuck Gleason and Jess Fritchie of Conejos.

“Relax, gents,” Chuck advised. “They won’t show up till night time, maybe not till early tomorrow.”

“Maybe not at all,” growled Sheriff Fritchie.

“Betcha on it,” Tony said confidently. What made him sure was a new padlock on the gate. For unless the thieves intended to use this place again, why would they provide it with a new lock? A lock with enough keys, no doubt, for all who brought horses here and all who took them away.

“Whenever they show up,” Chuck drawled, “it’s us or them. Van dibs on the first shot at Trigger Huggins.”

Two rides later, up at the Alamosa celebration, Margie heard the voice of Blaise Amory at her elbow. " 'Scuse me a minute, ladies. I'll be right back."

He'd been with them for the last hour, occasionally commenting on the form of the competing riders. Now he strode away, tall, creamy hat aslant and spurs jingling. Blaise himself, later in the day, was billed to exhibit his trained stallion.

He angled across the grounds toward a cluster of wagons and tents. Country families who couldn't afford hotels were camping there. Back of a deserted wagon Amory joined the small, goat-smelling man who'd beckoned from a distance.

The man looked frightened. He stood by the horse on which he'd ridden hard from Conejos. "It is important," he said huskily. "So I leave my goats and come fast."

Amory glanced warily right and left. "Spill it, Cimino."

"As you know, *patrón*, my wife she is cook at the sheriff's house in Conejos."

Amory nodded impatiently. It was one of the reasons why he'd chosen Leo Cimino for his listening post there. "Go on."

"Yesterday she sets an extra plate because a guest eats with the sheriff. He is the cowboy Darrow. And as my woman serves them more mutton, she sees this cowboy show to the sheriff a padlock. It is the same padlock, *patrón*, which I myself have throw away in the creek."

Amory took an iron grip on his arm. "Are you sure?"

"There can be no doubt," the goatman insisted. "And when they are finish eating they ride away south."

It was enough for Amory. He couldn't doubt that a trap was laid, this very minute, at the padlocked gate. "Look, Cimino. Get yourself a fresh horse. Then burn the trail to the state line. You can head 'em off there. Huggins and Mock and Wycross. Tell 'em to turn the drive loose and scatter it. Have 'em hightail straight back to Alamosa."

"It is done, *patrón*." Cimino darted away.

Amory went back to the awning shelter and found Mark McCarron there. McCarron was congratulating Ed Murdy for a riding prize the Jaybird foreman had just won. Margie and Helga joined in and Murdy stood hat in hand, awkwardly embarrassed. " 'T'wan't nothin', ma'am," he mumbled, and seemed aware only of Helga.

"Just got word," Blaise Amory broke in, "that a man's waiting for me at the hotel. A hay deal, I think. So if you'll excuse me, Margie . . ." He touched his hat, gave Murdy a comradely backslap and left them.

His big stallion was at a tie rack close by and Amory rode at a gallop to the corner of Front and Hunt. He dropped the reins in front of the Victoria Hotel and crossed to the bank.

The assistant cashier stepped up cordially. "Hello, Mr. Camp," Amory said to him. "I need a paper out of my box, please."

The bank hadn't yet installed private lock boxes. But important customers like Blaise Amory were allowed to furnish metal boxes of their own and keep them in the vault. Mr. Camp now took Amory to the vault and from it brought out a small iron box. The only key in existence was one on Amory's keyring.

After unlocking the box he took a single paper from it. "Thanks, Mr. Camp." Blaise Amory crossed back to the hotel and went up to his permanent room there.

Behind a locked door he stared bitterly at what he'd brought from the bank box. It was a warranty deed conveying nineteen parcels of land from George Chester to Blaise Amory. Each parcel was a choice quarter section of water-fed land. One forged deed transferred all of them from Chester, who didn't exist, to Amory, who did, and the deed had been notarized by Saul Spengler.

Amory had planned to wait at least a year before putting the deed on record. Best if the entry didn't appear too close, by dates, to the nineteen deeds from as many patentees to George Chester. He himself, by messenger, could keep up Chester's taxes. And meantime he could keep building up his reputation as a speculator with the habit of picking up odd land bargains here and there.

But now, he conceded dismally, the whole scheme had blown up in his face. The exposure of Trinidad Jones would bring about a thorough scrutiny of the county records. The result would make the ghost name, Chester, smell to high heaven. He didn't dare record a deed which would link his name to Chester's.

And now this tip about a trap at the padlocked gate made things immeasurably worse. It meant Tony Darrow knew about the periodic horse drives to a turn-over station there. Rio Arriba County records, when searched, would show that George Chester owned the canyon. Which would tie the name Chester to both horse stealing and murder, because in a chase after thieves a year ago a bullet had killed Tommy McCarron.

Margie's brother! So a link to Chester would mean losing Margie herself—and perhaps his own neck!

But suddenly Blaise Amory, his wits always nimble and resilient, saw a way out of it. A way in which he could destroy this deed and still salvage its value! A way to hold and keep the fruit of his schemings, uncontaminated by the name of Chester, and win every stake including Margie McCarron.

A gleam fired Blaise Amory's eye. His mind

worked out every detail. Then he struck a match and held it to a warranty deed. Title to three thousand watered acres, worth thirty thousand dollars, burned to an ash in his hand.

16

Night brought a blaze of lights to the Perry House. Mark McCarron sat in the lobby and watched gayly costumed couples stream through and into the dining room. This would be the most extravagant ball ever held in Alamosa.

Some came as courtiers and some as pirates; there were ladies in colonial gowns and powdered hair.

John Moomaw's band struck up its liveliest tune, mingling melody with laughter and banter from the floor. For a pleasant hour Mark McCarron sat chewing his cigar, looking on, occasionally exchanging greetings with some neighbor. He remembered the last frolic he'd attended here. A problem had troubled him then—Tony Darrow and Margie's growing attachment for him.

Now that was all settled and over. Darrow was out of it. Blaise Amory was Margie's one and only romance. This very minute she was dancing with Blaise; and a glimpse of her proved to McCarron that she was quite happy about it. Certainly she was cured of Tony Darrow.

Cured of him, McCarron supposed, partly because of the stupidly implausible charges which Tony had blurted out against Blaise

Amory. And partly, perhaps, because Tony Darrow had twice this season killed a man in gunplay. Tully in Alamosa and Trinidad Jones at Conejos. And while in each case both the law and public opinion had exonerated Tony, a killing was still a killing. A dainty, extremely feminine girl like Margie would naturally shy away from a cowboy gunman. Especially one who, whether justly or unjustly, had served a term in prison.

So Tony Darrow, in McCarron's book, was ancient history. Current history was Blaise Amory.

Music came to an end and a few of the couples drifted out into the lobby, where it was cooler and where there was room for intimate talk. One of these was Ed Murdy and Helga Tarber, a handsome, well-matched pair, McCarron thought; Murdy as a leather-clad mountain man and Helga, with only wisps of her yellow hair peeping from under a mantilla, as a stately damosel of old Spain. Well apart from them stood Margie, a high-combed coquette of Madrid smiling over her fan at Juan Bautista de Anza, who a hundred years ago had governed all the vast province from here to the Pacific Ocean, and who tonight was Blaise Amory of the Jaybird ranch.

A voice startled McCarron. A guttural voice with a challenge in it, and he turned to see an iron-visaged Ute Indian standing erect by his chair. That in itself wasn't too strange, for an Indian was a common sight on the streets of Alamosa.

But this one was pointing toward Margie and Amory. "Woman girl belong you?" he inquired.

"She's my daughter." Annoyance furrowed McCarron's brow.

"Her happy now," stated Unahwa the Ute. "Some day woman girl plenty sad."

McCarron half rose from his chair. "Sad about what?" he demanded.

"Him!" Unahwa spoke like an oracle and his smoldering black eyes burned a stare at Blaise Amory. "Him not good for woman girl. Him kill many men. Him speak with the forked tongue."

Without waiting for an answer the Indian left the lobby and was gone from sight. It left McCarron petrified with shock, indignant anger—and finally with creeping misgivings. And an uncanny sensation that much the same thing had happened before.

Only the other time, at a Perry House ball such as this, an anonymous note had told tales on Tony Darrow.

All that night McCarron couldn't sleep. He tossed restlessly in his hotel room, confusion and doubt growing by the hour. All his hopes for Margie's future had been built on Blaise Amory. And now . . . but time and again he shook off the gnawing doubt and called himself a fool. Why should he get all stirred up by the mutterings of an illiterate Ute?

Could it be the same one, McCarron wondered, who'd been mentioned cryptically by Tony Darrow to the editor of the Alamosa weekly? Maybe the Indian had an old grudge against Amory; maybe for revenge he'd first poisoned Tony's mind toward Amory and was now shooting the same arrow at McCarron!

The Wagon Wheel owner had breakfast early and alone. At the desk he left a note for Margie telling her he planned to stay in town all day. The girls could send for the buckboard and drive it to the ranch.

To think it through, and perhaps catch another glimpse of the mysterious Indian, McCarron went out and walked the streets of Alamosa. He'd get to the bottom of it, McCarron resolved fiercely, or know why. He'd shake whatever sullen motive the Indian had, whether real or imaginary, out of him.

After looking in every dive along Front, McCarron doubled back along Fifth. He even tramped to an *alamosa* on the river bank where bands of Indians sometimes camped. Then he stood for an hour at Blackmore's corral, on Denver Street, merely because he noticed some Indian ponies there.

But when a group of Ute skin traders came for

the ponies, the mystery man of last night wasn't among them.

Frustration pricked at McCarron as he tramped back to State Avenue. He found Milt Yeager at the marshal's office. "Haven't seen a Ute buck around town, have you, Milt? Man with a black felt hat and a hawk feather in it."

"Not that I recollect, Mark. But there was a heck of a crowd in town yesterday."

The rancher crossed to the *Weekly Independent.* "Remember that interview you printed one time? About young Darrow tipping you to check on some Ute Indian. Ever catch up with him?"

The editor, accepting the cigar McCarron offered, shook his head. "Don't believe there is any such Indian, Mark. Chances are Darrow just pulled him out of a hat."

At the Perry House McCarron learned that the girls had sent for the rig and were now on their way home. He sat down in a lobby rocker and stared moodily across Front. A switch engine over there was bunting little narrow-gauge cattle cars up a siding. The bawlings of penned cattle came to McCarron in varied tones—deep bellows of steers in protest against shipment and the high-pitched plaints of weaning calves.

An ox-drawn wagon stopped at the trough in front of Slavick's, the oxen sucking water there while the driver went inside for a draught of his own. A cavalryman from Fort Garland, straight-backed and young in his McClellan saddle, cantered cockily by.

Then McCarron saw Blaise Amory. Amory striding west along the Front Street walk and his face seemed tautly preoccupied. He passed the hotel and went on up Front toward San Juan.

An impulse gripped McCarron. Why not be as frank with Blaise as he'd been with Tony Darrow? He'd called Tony into the parlor and asked bluntly for an explanation. Why not overtake Blaise and ask what connection he'd had, if any, with a sore-headed Ute? No doubt Blaise would give a reason which at once would clear the air.

McCarron went out and hurried west up the sidewalk, catching sight of Amory a block ahead. He quickened his step and after crossing San Juan he saw Amory turn into a saloon further on.

The place, McCarron noted with shock and amazement, was Brophy's Bar. It shocked him because on a minor point it partially confirmed one of the wild charges made by Tony Darrow. A charge that a quartette of thug killers hung out there and a hint that they operated at the beck and call of Blaise Amory.

McCarron hurried on, disturbed and cautious now, and when he came to the twin half-doors of Brophy's entrance he did not at once go in. He stood on the walk and looked over the doors. A filthy place of vile smells and inside he saw the backwash of Alamosa. It was no fit place for a rancher of standing like Amory.

Yet there stood Amory, alone at midbar, lifting a neat rye to his lips. He spoke to no one, looked at no one. After downing half the rye, he rolled a cigaret with care and precision. This he lighted. But after a puff or two he tossed it away.

McCarron saw it land in the sawdust at a rear table where four men sat at cards. One of the players raked it toward him with his boot, stamped it out, leaned over to pick it up. What he did with it McCarron had no chance to see. For Blaise Amory swallowed the rest of his liquor and abruptly left the saloon.

McCarron barely missed a collision. He did so by darting to one side and into a pool hall next door. Amory didn't see him. When the coast was clear McCarron came out, hating himself for a skulking spy, and took an opposite direction.

But after circling the block and stopping for a quick one at Slavick's, certain unpleasant realities popped up to torment McCarron. A barful of witnesses had gossiped about a run-in between Tony Darrow and four toughies at Brophy's. And while the story was garbled by too many repetitions, in substance it was that Amory, according to Darrow, had twice flipped a murder message concealed in a half-smoked cigaret. The first resulting in death to Pancho Morales and the second in a hole through Tony's hat.

McCarron himself had seen the hole in Tony's hat.

But still, he argued stubbornly, it didn't prove a thing. Any man at a bar is likely to throw away a cigaret. And any bum in a barroom is likely to pick it up. "Shooting snipes" was the term for it. McCarron, who chewed cigars without smoking them, had time and again thrown them away; time and again he'd seen vagrants pick them up.

He'd almost succeeded in rationalizing the incident when five cowboys galloped down State Avenue. They stopped at the trough in front of Slavick's. Five solid affidavits in the flesh, McCarron thought, of Amory's integrity. For this was the entire Jaybird crew led by the foreman, Ed Murdy. Square-shooters, all of them, not the kind to hire out to any but a square-shooting employer.

They were a badge of Amory's respectability and McCarron went out to the trough for a neighborly greeting. "Hello, Ed. In to spend that prize money you won yesterday?"

Murdy grinned. "Not a chance, Mr. McCarron. We got to pound leather all the way to the Zapata ranch and look at some heifers. Boss figgers they might be a bargain and he wants our vote on it."

The five riders took off in a cloud of dust, heading toward the dunes of singing sands.

Uncertainty again fretted McCarron. Why should Amory send his *entire* crew on an errand like that? It would be sundown when they got there, so they couldn't possibly inspect cattle and return home before late tomorrow. Was Amory getting rid of them overnight? And why?

In the late afternoon McCarron rode soberly toward his own ranch. While saddling up at the livery barn he'd noticed Amory's sorrel in the next stall. So he knew Amory was still in town.

Which meant that no one was on the Jaybird except a Chinese cook.

McCarron came presently to Alamosa Creek. He was about to leave the main road there and turn right toward the Wagon Wheel when he saw a buggy coming up a trail from the left. The buggy had one slow-gaited horse and the driver was Chinese. Suspicion tugged again at McCarron and he waited.

"Howdy, Wong. Going to town?"

The Jaybird cook gave a delighted cackle. "Yessee please. Boss send word me meet train. Hay buyer come along from Pueblo. Me meet him take him home to ranch." The buggy, now on the main road, creaked on toward Alamosa.

McCarron stared after it with grim calculations. The Pueblo train didn't get here till an hour after dark. It would take at least three hours for a slow buggy to get back to the La Jara Creek ranch. Which would leave the ranch entirely deserted till midnight.

Had Amory called a meeting there? A meeting

of thieves and murderers? Had a message in a cigaret called the meeting? If so where would it be except at Amory's own ranch, from which he'd carefully cleared away every honest pair of ears?

Decision came to McCarron. Margie's happiness was at stake. And there was only one place to find out the truth. Instead of reining right toward his own ranch, he reined left toward Amory's.

17

Amory got home an hour before dark and loosed his stallion in the corral. At the house Wong had set out a cold supper for him. The Jaybird man ate calmly, his golden-brown face relaxed now, while overhead whippoorwills called in the twilight.

As dark came on he lighted a blue-shaded oil lamp and put it in a window. This was the all-clear signal he'd used for years. Not that he planned to receive foul-smelling men like Pinky Mock here in the house. A house kept immaculate by Wong whose sensitive nose and eye would quickly detect any contamination or disarrangement. Nor did Amory want the Pinky Mock ilk sitting around on plush cushions in a house which some day would be presided over by Margie McCarron.

The barn was a more suitable place for Mock and Wycross and Huggins.

So Amory took a lantern to the barn and set it on a grain box in the saddle rack vestibule. He provided no drinks. They could do their guzzling at Brophy's. And since Wong would be back in a few hours, to report that a hay buyer had failed to arrive on the train, the quicker this meeting was over the better.

Hoofbeats drummed up the lane and four

horsemen emerged from the night. One who looked like a Spanish gentleman, a long serape thrown over his shoulder, and three who looked like gringo thugs. They dismounted and came into the barn vestibule to find Amory sitting on a staple box there.

"What goes?" squeaked Pinky Mock.

"That's what I wanta know," came throatily from Wycross. "We had thirty head on a fast lope for New Mex when Leo Cimino flagged us down. Worth real dough, them broncs, but Leo said let 'em go."

"If you hadn't, you'd be feeding the buzzards by now." Amory waved a hand toward the saddle racks and three of the men took perches on them. Only Diego Sandoval remained standing, his lips sucking daintily at a corn-shuck cigaret.

Amory looked at him with a grudging admiration. "You're just as cold-blooded now, Diego, as you were the night we mopped up on Pablo Arragon."

"What goes?" again demanded Pinky Mock.

"Everything," Amory broke it to them bluntly. "We can't run off any more horse stock, because the law's wise to the canyon where Augie Squiers picks them up. We can't file on any more land, because that play turned toes up with Trinidad Jones. We can't even keep the three thousand acres already proved up. In fact I've burned the deed."

"The hell you have!" exploded Trigger Huggins. Mock too let out a howl and Wycross erupted: "All that trouble for nothing! You said we'd clean up. You said . . ."

"I said there were risks," Amory cut in. "A risk of someone trying to run out on us, like Pancho Morales. A risk of someone flubbing his disguise, like Trinidad Jones. A risk of bumping into some smart guy like Tony Darrow. But keep your shirts on. There's still a way. A way to ditch the land and still cash in."

A sullen silence. Then Diego's soft voice. "We are listening, señor."

Amory dropped his cigaret and tamped it with his boot. "Look, men. For a year now Augie Squiers has had a gripe. He claims our end of it pays off better than his. You've heard him."

"Plenty times," Huggins said. "He hollers his head off. Claims he's got figgers to prove it."

"His figures," Amory summed up, "are like this. He gets the horses and we get the land. So far we've proved up on three thousand acres of handpicked bottomland worth, he claims, ten dollars an acre. Which is thirty thousand dollars. His end has been horses which he's sold for enough cash to stock his H Bar ranch at Walsenburg with four hundred cows. The cows are worth thirty a head, he claims, or twelve thousand pesos. So his gripe is we've out-earned him thirty to twelve."

"And now," Wycross growled, "we ain't got nothin' and he's got the cows."

Yet a sly confidence on Amory's face held their attention. "Look, since he's dissatisfied, let's trade ends with him. Let him take title to the land and I'll take title to the cows. Let him find out later there's a flaw in any title which can be traced back to George Chester."

Only the intelligent dark eyes of Sandoval seemed to grasp it. "*Magnifico*!" the Spaniard applauded under his breath. The others only gaped.

Amory snapped at them impatiently. "Must I draw you a diagram? I tore up Chester's deed to myself because I don't dare put it on record. So I'll have Spengler notarize another one giving title to Squiers. I take it to Walsenburg and trade it for four hundred cows. I ship two hundred to Denver for cash to pay you men off. I ship the other two hundred to Alamosa and stock the Jaybird with them. What can be simpler than that?"

Nothing, they agreed finally, could be simpler. Augie Squiers, when he recorded a George Chester deed, would be pounced upon by U. S. land officers. But his own neck would pay the penalty if he told tales on Amory. Nor could anything on record entangle Amory.

"Who's ridin' herd on Saul Spengler," Mock wanted to know, "since Trinidad got lead-poisoning?"

"Fella named Lew Wager," Amory told them. "He's safe, because he hates the law and he hates Tony Darrow. We don't have to cut him in. Happens he needs a hideout himself so he doesn't mind lying low with Spengler. I didn't tell him a thing except that keeping Spengler out of circulation means bad luck for Tony Darrow. Seems Darrow stymied a trick of his one time."

Pinky chuckled. "Right now Darrow's ridin' the skin off his saddle lookin' fer Spengler up around Placer. All because I started a rumor Saul was seen in a Placer bar."

Amory grinned his approval. For Spengler's present hideout was a hundred miles from Placer. "Pinky, you better burn everything at the Los Mogotes cache. We won't need it any more."

"Every hair of it," Mock promised. At the Los Mogotes cache were the dozen disguises in which he and others had appeared periodically before a clerk of a county court with homestead applications and proof papers. "We sure fooled 'em for a while," Mock chuckled.

Actually more than sixty claims had been filed by mail in the San Luis and San Juan valleys. Of these nineteen had been patented, seven had been canceled due to suspicion of bad faith or fraud, while some forty had been pending at the time of the last ill-fated attempt by Trinidad Jones.

Blaise Amory shrugged. "It's water over the dam. So we settle for four hundred cows. While

I go after them, Diego, you'd better team up with Huggins."

"It will be a pleasure," purred Sandoval. Since May, Huggins' main assignment had been the sniping of Tony Darrow.

"He's living on borrowed time," Trigger bragged. "I've had him in my sights two-three times."

"Get going," Amory directed, "before my China boy comes home."

From cottonwoods along La Jara Creek came the neigh of a horse. The sound startled Amory. Four saddled horses stood in front of the barn. His own horses were either coralled or in an upvalley pasture. "Wait here," he muttered uneasily, "while I take a look."

He was gone five minutes and when he came back the golden-brown of his face had turned cloudy gray. "It's a Wagon Wheel horse. The one Mark McCarron always rides. Saddled and tied in the creek brush not a hundred yards from this barn!"

"*Caramba*!" murmured Diego Sandoval.

"A snooper huh?" blurted Wycross.

Amory snapped fast orders. "Pick him up. Mock, you beat the brush around this house. Wycross, look in all the outshacks. Circle the house, Huggins. Diego, light another lantern and look in the loft. I'll cover the grain room and the stalls."

They scattered. But five minutes later a call from Sandoval assembled them in the barn vestibule. Mark McCarron, with loft hay clinging to his coat, stood with Diego's gun aimed at his middle.

Amory and the others grouped eerily about him. McCarron stood stiffly defiant, the lantern light making yellow splotches on his face. No one said anything for a minute. Then Pinky Mock's squeaky voice cut the silence. "This kinda cooks up your weddin', don't it, Blaise? If he got a earful, you ain't likely to walk down no church aisle with that gal o' his."

Amory's look shut him up. Then McCarron began talking. Not angrily or fearfully, but sadly. "And I fired Tony Darrow! I sent him away and put *you* in his place! I treated you like a son, Blaise. I believed in you and so did Margie. Now I know Tony told the truth; so did the Indian. You'll murder me, I suppose, just like you murdered Pablo Arragon!"

"I wouldn't, Mark, if I knew any other way out." Amory's eyes slithered sideways to avoid McCarron's steady gaze. He looked at four men who waited for his decision. His skin turned a sick yellow and his voice faded to a mumble. "What else can we do, Mark? You shouldn't have come here. You shouldn't put me on a spot like this. . . ."

Trigger Huggins' voice broke in and a touch

of scorn in it wasn't for McCarron but for Blaise Amory. "Guess I'll have to do it for you, Blaise, same as usual."

McCarron turned as the triggerman and his gun spoke. The look of sad incredulity was still in his eyes as he crumpled slowly to the barn floor.

18

Summitville perched sky-high on the continental divide, fifty steep miles west of Alamosa. Gold and silver strikes had boomed it until the place now had six saloons, two mills, five stores and a summer population of a thousand. In winter it was locked from the world by deep snow,

Blaise Amory, today riding a brown gelding, stopped at one of the saloons. There he bought a gallon of whisky, dropped it in a sack and tied the sack to his saddle pommel. He rode on down a fir ridge toward Lookout Mountain and came, after a few miles, to an abandoned silver shaft with a cabin by it. Here was one of those false alarm strikes common to the San Juans. Amory had bought the place for a song; at present it made a good hideout; and some day it could be a summer cattle camp for the Jaybird ranch.

As he dismounted, Lew Wager came from the cabin. "He's asleep." Wager eyed the sack. "What you got there?"

"Rations for him," Amory said. "Put it out of sight. Feed him just enough to keep him contented but not enough to throw him into tremens."

A curious smirk rode Wager's beefy, small-eyed face. It was a week unshaven and made him as unkempt as any tramp. "What's the play, anyway?"

"Tell you later," Amory promised, although he had no intention of doing so. "Right now put away that sack and take a walk."

He waited till Wager was out of sight before going in to shake Saul Spengler. The notary sat up, bloated and bleary, grosser than he'd ever seemed before. Amory had nothing but contempt for the man. "Get out your seal, Saul."

"Pour me one first," Spengler begged. His voice was like a wire sawing on sandpaper.

"Notarize me a deed first. Then you can have all you want."

Amory had already filled out a warranty deed form, making it an exact copy of the one he'd burned except that the name of August Squiers was substituted for his own. "Augie and I made a little trade. He'll take the land and I'll take the stock."

That part of it made no difference to Spengler. Notarizing deeds, at the whim of Blaise Amory, had become routine with him. Without protest he put his seal on this one, painfully signing his name, then adding a date after the phrase, "My commission expires . . ."

"A drink," he pleaded, and Amory gave him a stiff one.

Amory rode down the mountain to Jasper and from there took the stage road toward Alamosa. It was dark when he hit the valley floor and soon after that he came opposite lighted windows of the Wagon Wheel ranch. He was tempted to stop in for an evening with Margie. Then he remembered a paper in his pocket—a deed bearing George Chester's name and notarized by Saul Spengler. It was a thing he must be rid of with a minimum of delay. His very possession of it could entangle him with Chester and Spengler.

So Amory spurred on, not to his own ranch but to Alamosa.

When the eastbound train left at eight in the morning he was on it. From a coach window he watched a sagy landscape slide by. For the first dozen miles the track paralleled a wagon road which came down from the Mosca Pass toll gate. A covered wagon crawled sluggishly along toward Alamosa. Further on the train passed another one. And still another. The wagon wheels kept rolling west.

In a few years more, Amory thought, San Luis Park would be dotted with cabins and brown sod would turn black under the plow. The incoming wagons he passed now made evidence of this and came as an ironic consolation to Amory. They convinced him that he could not in any case have carried on his scheme of ghost filings very much longer. A remote and isolated quarter section, surrounded by vacant lands, had a chance to escape publicity and inspection. There'd be no curious neighbor to spread tales.

But from now on, as the range filled up with settlers, the chance of a sneak proof on land would grow less and less. So the demise of Trinidad Jones, and of the mythical Chester, perhaps wasn't such a loss after all.

The train stopped at Fort Garland where Amory saw a few Indians and a sheepherder from the big Grant mingling with off-duty soldiers. A man with a badge on his shirt waved a hand and Amory recognized Sheriff Billy Carson of San Luis.

From here on the grade steepened as the engine chugged up a twisting gulch. Presently it stopped at Placer—half a mile of saloons and cabins strung along the track. The place was on the bulge of a gold boom, its summer population matching Alamosa's. While the train hooked on a pusher Amory glimpsed a cowboy at the tie rack of the Blue Front saloon. He looked tired and discouraged—as jaded as the calico pony whose reins he held. Tony Darrow! Sight of him brought a derisive smile to Amory. Darrow up this way hunting for Saul Spengler—on a trick tip planted by Pinky Mock!

With Spengler atop the opposite wall of the park, a three-day saddle ride from here!

As the train moved on, crawling torturously now up a four percent grade to the pass, Amory realistically considered Spengler. Spengler was his biggest hazard. The man would sell his soul for a drink, in fact had often done so. If Amory could buy him by appeasing his thirst, so perhaps could the law or Tony Darrow. So Spengler must be gotten rid of the minute he was no longer needed.

There was a bare chance he might be needed just once more. The chance was that Augie Squiers, at Walsenburg tomorrow, might balk at the trade Amory would offer. In which case Amory must find someone else on whom to saw off the George Chester titles. Once he'd completely disposed of them, he'd pay one last call on Saul Spengler.

But Augie Squiers, at his H Bar ranch near Walsenburg, didn't balk. For a long time he'd been disgruntled about getting the short end of a partnership. Thirty thousand dollars' worth of land looked a lot better to him than twelve thousand dollars' worth of cows.

His only question: "How come you changed your mind, Blaise?"

Amory's answer was prepared in advance. "I need some quick cash, Augie, to get in on the ground floor of a big ditch deal that'll spread Rio Grande water all over the park." Actually such a gigantic irrigation project was being promoted and the Denver papers had been full of it. "Cows turn quicker than land, Augie. I'd have to peddle those nineteen claims one at a time, and it'd take a year maybe. But cows are cash on the line."

All of which was true and Squiers knew it. He accepted a deed from George Chester to himself, officially notarized by Saul Spengler, and in return gave a bill of sale for four hundred cows. "Deliver 'em right away, Augie, to the railroad pens at Walsenburg."

Amory rode into Walsenburg and at the depot had the operator order twenty cattle cars—ten to go north to Denver and ten west to Alamosa. A day later the cattle were being loaded, twenty cows to the car. Amory sent two telegrams. One to a livestock commission company in Denver. They were to receive and market ten cars of cows, sending him the check in care of the bank at Alamosa. The other was to his foreman Ed Murdy.

AM ARRIVING WITH TEN CARS COWS—
MEET SHIPMENT WITH FULL CREW
AMORY

A sense of triumph tingled Amory as he stood by the Walsenburg siding and watched the northbound string of cars pull out for Denver. Then he boarded the caboose of the westbound string. A crushing weight was off him and he relaxed there, puffing a cigaret and exchanging quips with the freight crew. Only one hazard was left—

the loose tongue of Saul Spengler. He must get to Spengler at once.

Five others were expecting payoffs—Mock, Huggins, Wycross, Sandoval and Cimino. He'd stall them off, some way. The check hadn't arrived from Denver, he could say. When that excuse wore thin he'd think up another. Treachery was an art with Blaise Amory. Mock, Wycross and Cimino were small fry and wouldn't give him much trouble. Only Sandoval and Huggins were really tough. Short-changing that pair would need some finesse—and maybe a bit of luck.

Through the night the train climbed La Veta Pass and dawn found it coasting down into the park. At the Fort Garland stop Amory inspected his cars, found one heifer down and poked her to her feet with a pole. The cattle were bawling for water as they moved on toward Alamosa.

Ed Murdy and his crew were waiting at the pens there. Amory swung off the caboose and hailed them. "They're all yours, Ed. Unload 'em fast and drift 'em to the river bed. Let 'em graze easy and slow to the ranch."

"You look tuckered, boss. Better get yourself a feed and a drink."

Amory crossed Front Street and went into Slavick's. Slavick slid a Scotch highball to him. "That oughta pick you up, Blaise."

Amory had it halfway to his lips when he saw Lew Wager.

Wager haggard and thorn-scratched, much as Blaise Amory himself had been, six years ago, after his foot race from the Arragon massacre to Fort Garland. By his looks and bruises Wager might have come fully as far afoot this past day and night.

Amory carried his drink to a table, beckoned and Wager joined him there. “Wasn’t my fault,” the man pleaded. “He sneaked out on me while I was asleep.”

Amory wanted to choke him. But here in a respectable saloon like Slavick’s he couldn’t even cuff the man. “When was this?” he demanded.

“Night before last. In the morning he was gone with both horses. And a gallon of liquor. Saul Spengler, I mean.”

19

Tony Darrow rode into Alamosa on a fagged horse. He'd covered the entire area from Placer to Mosca Pass in a vain hunt for Spengler. His face had tired lines and was shaggy. After stabling his horse he went to a barber shop for a shave.

The shop was humming with talk.

"They can't find him nowhere."

"Every cow hand in the park's out lookin' fer him, I hear."

"That red-headed gal o' his's takin' it hard. His bronc comin' home without a saddle like that! Nobody's seen him since he started home the evenin' of the fifth."

"Just faded into thin air, Mark did."

In that way Tony learned about the disappearance of McCarron. "Funny thing, too," the barber said. "Everybody liked Mark. Nobody'd wanta hurt him. Unless somebody socked him for his wallet. He always carried a wad of money around."

"Blaise Amory's leadin' the search, I hear. Put every hand he's got in the saddle and told 'em to keep lookin' till they find McCarron."

Tony heard more of the same at the Victoria. He got a night's sleep and in the morning rode to his homestead on the Conejos. The cabin was now finished and equipped with the bare necessities for himself and Chuck Gleason. Tony pulled the latchstring and went in. A note in Chuck's handwriting lay on the table.

> TONY—Everybody's out looking for McCarron. They assigned me to Conejos Canyon between Los Mogotes and the mouth of La Manga. If you want to join me you'll find me camped about two mile above where Sheep Creek comes in—
>
> CHUCK

Tired as he was, no thought of evading the search occurred to Tony. Mark McCarron had fired him from a job. But Margie's distress was all the command he needed. After a bite to eat he caught up a fresh horse, tied a blanket roll back of the saddle and headed for Conejos Plaza.

Dark caught him there and he stayed all night at the little adobe hotel. Sheriff Fritchie was out looking for McCarron. But it was Blaise Amory, they told him, who by popular assent was in command of the search.

Tony was asaddle by daylight and riding up the Conejos. Its canyon proper began at foothills called Los Mogotes, and from there on Tony knew he was in the area assigned to Chuck Gleason. Twelve miles of timbered canyon whose steep walls rose higher with every mile.

Cottonwood and willow in the canyon bed and piny slopes on either side—a wild and unsettled gash in the San Juans.

Why would anyone hope to find McCarron here? Probably they didn't, but had given Chuck this stretch because he'd volunteered, and because every inch of the region must be covered.

A thought made Tony rein to a stop. Barber shop chatter came back to him. "Blaise Amory leading the search." If Amory was in command, then it was he who'd assigned Chuck to this particular neck of the park.

Tony took off his hat and looked at a bullet hole through it. He glanced up to woody slopes on either side. What a spot for a sniper like Huggins! If only Huggins knew he was here!

Riding on, Tony's mind sparked over every angle. Huggins could know Chuck Gleason was here, but Trigger Huggins was gunning for Tony, not Gleason. Yet Gleason had left a note on the cabin table—a cabin whose out-hanging latchstring barred no one. Trigger's mission was to ambush and kill Tony Darrow. Reasonably he'd scout Tony's homestead whenever it was deserted—scout it to learn Tony's whereabouts and plans. A look there yesterday would have exposed Chuck's note.

At this point the trail ran along the south bank of the river. Tony left it and forded to the other side. He rode his horse up the piny slope and high above the river he found a game path. This gave poor footing for a horse. So Tony got off and led the animal. Constantly his eyes scanned the canyon floor below.

It made slow going. Occasionally the steepness forced him to a detour. A buck leaped from the aspens and flashed quickly out of sight. Further on Tony came to a high shoulder which gave a view of the canyon ahead.

Looking obliquely down he saw two men. They lay on their stomachs behind a gravel bank a short way upcanyon. He could see only their backs. But each had a rifle and they peered over the bank in a downtrail direction. For here the main canyon road, which had followed the south bank of the river, now crossed to the north. A man riding upcanyon could easily be cut down by riflemen waiting behind the gravel bank.

Presently one of the two men got to his knees to light a cigaret. As he cupped a match against the wind Tony had a profile view of him. It was a corn-husk cigaret and the man was Diego Sandoval.

Sandoval who'd once said: "Some day I will kill you, señor."

The other man was sure to be Huggins. From this vantage it would be easy to pick them off. Instead Tony retreated a little way and then rode his horse still further up the slope. Almost at its ridge he found another game path and used it to detour the men below. They were waiting for him, of course. But he couldn't prove it. Least of all could he prove they'd been posted there by Blaise Amory.

A feeling of frustration drew Tony's lips to a grim tight line as he slid back into the canyon. He was now half a mile above the ambushers, too far for them to hear sliding gravel. At the river level he resumed his way up its pools and riffles, coming presently to a bedroll and saddle under the cottonwoods. It was Chuck's saddle. Warm coffee in a can on fire ashes meant Chuck wasn't far away. This bend in the Conejos, a shady grove by a foam-flecked pool, made a fine campsite. Tony hunkered on his spurs there and in a little while Chuck appeared with a pair of fat trout on a forked willow.

"Caught 'em with a grasshopper." He grinned. "Fan up the fire, cowboy."

While trout sizzled Tony told him about the ambush a mile below. "So I by-passed 'em, Chuck. Nothing to gain by gunning it out with 'em."

"The heck there ain't!" Gleason was outraged. "After we fill 'em fulla lead, they won't be waitin' at the next gulch you happen to ride by. Load your gun, cowboy, and let's whang into 'em."

Tony was in a mood to temporize. "Suppose we fill 'em fulla lead! Like you say. What do we do with 'em then?"

"That's easy. We pack 'em down to Conejos and say: 'Here you are, sheriff, a coupla two-timin' dry-gulchers who was tryin' to . . .' "

Chuck came to a sputtering stop and Tony asked: "Tryin' to do what, Chuck? All we can say is they were lyin' back of a gravel bank with loaded rifles. Maybe they were huntin' me, maybe they were huntin' deer."

"Huntin' deer my eye!" Gleason snorted. "They're Blaise Amory's triggermen and it was Blaise who put me in this neck o' the woods. They figgered you'd follow me so they laid a trap. Dagged if I let 'em get away with it." Chuck went up the river and came back with his horse. He broke camp, threw on a saddle, crammed his rifle into the scabbard. "They want a fight, they can sure have one!"

"We'll close in quietly," Tony consented reluctantly, "and get 'em covered. Then we'll tell 'em to hightail outa the canyon."

They rode downtrail, stirrup to stirrup, at a cautious walk. "How do you figure this McCarron business?" Tony asked.

"It throws me," Chuck admitted. "Amory wouldn't have anything to do with it, seems like, him bein' a friend of McCarron's. But he's sure makin' time with Margie, right now, takin' charge of this search. Rides around like a general givin' orders. Puts an arm around Margie, comfortin'-like. 'Don't you cry, little girl; I'll find him.' Biggest grandstander I ever see, that guy is."

"We're getting close," Tony warned.

They dismounted, took rifles from saddle boots and went on afoot. Tony knew just where to look, and soon they were peering from a thicket only thirty yards from the ambush. Sandoval and Huggins still lay face-down behind a gravel bank, in a position to bush-whack anyone riding upriver from Conejos.

The cowboys moved softly forward, each with a ready rifle. But a rifle could be an awkward weapon in close combat; so as he advanced Tony shifted his rifle to his left hand and dropped his right on the butt of his forty-five. Chuck did the same.

They were only ten paces away when Sandoval heard them. The Spaniard jumped to his feet and spun around with his rifle spitting. Trigger Huggins rolled to his left and skewed around on his knees, firing. A bullet nicked Chuck's sleeve and another fanned Tony's cheek. Both cowboys cut loose with their forty-fives, Tony firing only once, Chuck twice.

Huggins yelled as he went down. Diego Sandoval rocked slowly on his feet, dropped his rifle. He put a hand over his middle where Chuck's bullet had punched. But his bitter stare was for Tony Darrow. "My mistake, señor," he murmured, then doubled up beside Huggins.

• • •

Near sunset they rode into Conejos Plaza, Tony leading Sandoval's horse and Chuck leading Huggins'. The dead men were draped over their saddles. All of Conejos stared from its cantinas, its *tiendas baratas* and its flat-roofed adobe courthouse. Citizens came forth to group in awe in front of the sheriff's office.

"*Caramba*!" they exclaimed in whispers, eyes centering on Tony Darrow. "Is not this the same who killed Trinidad Jones? He has killed again, *primo*!"

Jess Fritchie listened gravely to Tony's account of the fight. His eyes squinted. "You say they fired first?"

"They sure did," Chuck broke in. "It was us or them, sheriff."

"If they fired first," Fritchie decreed, "you're in the clear. But if they didn't, you're not." He gave Tony a straight look. "There've been a few too many killings around this range. If I remember right, Darrow, you've had a hand in plenty of 'em."

"Some of them," Tony said, "didn't come off." He held his hat out to show the hole through it.

Coroner Celestino Romero appeared, as feather-voiced and polite as ever. "You can prove self-defense, I hope, señores?" His code was the same as Fritchie's.

Fritchie drew him aside for a discussion. The

sheriff's face had a stony set when he turned again to Tony. "Killings can get to be a habit," he said stiffly. "We've got too many Billy-the-Kids in this country and somethin's got to be done about it. If you can prove these dead men fired first . . ."

The blood crept up Tony's neck. "Chuck says they did and so do I. That's all the proof we got." The inference that he was another Billy-the-Kid, a saddle hoodlum who right now was terrorizing down in New Mexico some four counties south of here, bit deep. "They were lyin' back of a bank," he charged again, "to pot me as I rode upriver—and it was Blaise Amory who put 'em there!" The pitch of Tony's resentment catapulted the last from his lips.

Sheriff and coroner exchanged disapproving glances. The coroner tugged at his short goatee and shook his head sadly. Blaise Amory was something of a hero with him. Again the two officials conferred aside. Presently Fritchie announced the decision. "The coroner will hold an inquest tomorrow morning, and let a jury decide if it's self-defense homicide. I'm not juggin' you men, y' understand; but stay right here on the plaza till inquest time tomorrow."

A kick on the shin from Chuck checked Tony's retort. He followed Chuck to a barn where they left their horses. "Awful nice of 'em," Tony said bitterly, "not to slap us in jail!"

Chuck was a bit older and took it in stride. "It's a raw deal, *amigo.* But goin' on the prod won't help us any."

They took a room at the hotel, Tony chafing under the humiliation of it. News of the killings, and of his detention at the county seat, would spread all over the park. By morning Alamosa would know about it. So would Margie and Helga at the Wagon Wheel ranch. He was already in Margie's bad books; what would she think now? Helga would stand by him; she always had. But not Margie McCarron.

It didn't sting Chuck Gleason so much because he'd never spent two years in prison; so he didn't have Tony's sensitivity to arrest. "That's what it amounts to!" Tony said. " 'I'm not juggin' you men, y'understand.' " His tone mimicked Fritchie. " 'Just don't leave town.' "

Tony went to bed but couldn't sleep. According to the county officers, his only chance lay in proving the dead men had started the shooting. And that was impossible! The futility of it flogged Tony. Morning found him grim and haggard.

"And look at the crowd!" Chuck exclaimed as they left the hotel after breakfast. Every tie rack was full. People had swarmed in from ranch and hamlet to attend a double homicide inquest. "Bad news sure flies faster'n a buzzard on this range!"

Tony grimaced. "Guess I'm getting a reputation. That crack the sheriff made about Billy-the-Kid!"

"Let's keep our shirts on," Gleason counseled. "No jury'll jug us for knockin' over a coupla horse thieves like Sandoval and Huggins."

The flaw in that, Tony reasoned, was that no one could prove horse stealing against that pair. Tony himself had weakened the horse stealing case against them by organizing the misfire trap on July Fourth, at the padlocked canyon. After that fiasco his standing with Fritchie had taken an abrupt drop.

Fritchie and the coroner were waiting at the courthouse door. The sheriff was gazing fixedly into distance. "We've postponed it an hour," he announced.

"You mean the inquest?"

"Word has just come, señor," this in the soft voice of Celestino Romero, "that there was a witness. One who is now on his way here to testify about who fired the first shot."

Tony stared. "A witness? There was nobody within miles!"

"Here he comes now, señor. The witness." The coroner pointed and Tony followed his finger.

His shocked eyes saw Blaise Amory. The Jaybird man galloped across the plaza and reined to a stop in front of the courthouse steps. He swung his leg over the stallion's rump and dismounted with a flourish. His fine golden smile was all but hidden by a two-day growth of beard. Captaining the search for McCarron had put him that far behind in his shaving. Evidence of incessant hard riding through the brush was apparent in the scratches and tears on his shirt and vest.

He came up the steps with nods to Chuck, the sheriff and the coroner, his eyes ignoring Tony Darrow.

"*Buenos días, señor.*" Romero's greeting was almost unctuous. "Is it true that you witnessed the shooting yesterday afternoon?"

"I did," Amory affirmed, "if it happened at exactly two o'clock."

The sheriff looked at his notes. Two o'clock was the hour reported by Darrow and Gleason. "But look, Blaise. They's timber all around there. How could you see the fight unless you was right on the spot?"

The Jaybird man rubbed his stubbled cheek, smiling. "I didn't see it," he corrected. "I *heard* it."

"You heard it?"

"Gunfire carries a long way, sheriff, in a canyon where the other wall can throw back echoes. I was riding along the ridge between Fox Creek and the Conejos, at two o'clock yesterday, looking for sign of Mark McCarron. I heard shooting down on the Conejos. Didn't think anything of it. Two cowboys, maybe, one with a six-gun and one with a rifle, potting at game.

But now it's different. I know it was men against men."

Fritchie eyed him quizzically, nodding. "It sure was, Blaise. Huggins and Sandoval did their shooting with rifles; and the bullets we dug outa them came from six-guns. All we need to know now is which went off first, the six-guns or the rifles."

The coroner looked a bit doubtful. "But could you tell the difference by sound, señor?"

"You can be the judge of that," Amory suggested. "Let somebody shoot off the same guns over there behind Garcia's store."

Romero went inside and reappeared with the rifles which had belonged to Huggins and Sandoval. He then collected the forty-five hip guns of Darrow and Gleason. "I shall fire them myself," he announced. Lugging all four weapons he crossed the plaza and disappeared behind Alfredo Garcia's *tienda.*

Complete dismay possessed Tony. He didn't believe for a moment that Amory had heard the shots. Still, it was possible. The ridge between Fox Creek and the Conejos wasn't more than half a mile from the shooting. And everyone knew that Amory had been scouring the country for McCarron. So the build-up was perfect. Amory need only swear that six-guns had fired before rifles—and a noose would be woven for Tony's neck.

At least fifty men were grouped in front of the steps. Every ear was cocked. Every man there knew the significance of the test.

From back of Garcia's store came four reports of gunfire. The first two were sharp cracks; the second pair were dull, thudding roars.

"The long guns fired first," Fritchie said instantly. And a dozen voices confirmed him.

"The gunplay in the canyon," Blaise Amory testified with suave certainty, "came in that same order. Two rifle shots; then pistol shots."

Tony gaped at him. Had he heard rightly? For the man's testimony completely vindicated him. Apology was already printed on Fritchie's face. The coroner rejoined them with a sheepish smile. "That is all the inquest we need, señores. The case is dismissed. Our thanks, Señor Amory."

Blaise Amory's eyes, turned now for the first time on Tony, were frankly unfriendly. "I don't owe this man any good will, sheriff. But it was my duty to tell what I knew." He went down the steps and swung into his saddle. "If you'll excuse me I'll start riding again. Can't stop till we find McCarron."

He spurred the stallion and galloped north toward the Wagon Wheel—and Margie McCarron.

20

Tony and Chuck rode silently out of town. They were a mile down the Conejos before Tony broke into bitter laughter. "Saved by Blaise Amory! Can you beat that? There we were, about to be hung, when up gallops Amory and does a one-man rescue. Is your head burning, Chuck?"

"What with?"

"Coals of fire."

They jogged another silent mile. Chuck brooded through two cigarets. "Why would he make a play like that, *amigo*? It ain't like him."

"It's a play for Margie," Tony concluded. "And the smartest one he ever made. Women go for these big-hearted, noble men. The kind that return good for evil. There I was, callin' him names, and he kills me with kindness. Watch it go over big with Margie."

They unsaddled at the homestead cabin and Tony spent a day and night catching up on sleep. On the second morning Ed Murdy stopped by. Ed was thin-drawn and tired, having ridden for days in the organized, parkwide search for McCarron.

"Fifty men have been out," Murdy reported wearily, "and Blaise assigned each of us to a sector. You'd think we'd at least find McCarron's saddle."

The idea of a dragnet managed by Amory stirred Tony with an idea. Alone with Chuck he gave it words. "Fifty men lookin' for McCarron might stumble on to Saul Spengler. Spengler's the key to Amory's deviltry. So Amory doesn't want anybody trippin' over Spengler."

"I'm listenin'," Chuck prompted. "So what?"

"So Amory, assigning fifty men to sectors, skips one of them. Either skips it or assigns it to himself. The one he skips is the one that hides Spengler."

"Maybe you got somethin'," Chuck said. "Let's take a ride to the Wagon Wheel and see what we can find out."

"One thing we'll find out," Tony predicted wryly, "is that I'm knee-high to a duck with Margie." They saddled and rode westerly, crossing the rail track at the La Jara Creek trestle.

Only Sam Akin was at the Wagon Wheel bunkhouse. He'd come by for a fresh horse. "Who's ridin' where?" Chuck asked him.

A map of San Luis Park was tacked on the wall and Akin thumbed toward it. "There's what Blaise calls his master plan. It's to keep us from trippin' over one another, Blaise says."

On the map Tony saw lines and names. Chuck's name was written in Conejos Canyon above Los Mogotes. Fifty other names were spotted methodically over the park. Amory had assigned himself no sector at all.

“He sure give you a break, Tony.” Akin grinned. “Gettin’ you outa that jamb at Conejos.”

“Who told you about it, Sam?”

“Who hasn’t? Everybody’s talkin’ about it. And it’s sure put Blaise in solid with little Miss Redhead up at the house. If it wasn’t she was grievin’ about her pa, I’d look fer weddin’ bells any day now.”

Tony looked across the ranch yard and saw Helga Tarber come out of the springhouse and walk toward the kitchen with a crock of cream. He hurried that way, catching her at the kitchen door.

“Tony!” Color mounted her cheeks but he couldn’t tell whether she was annoyed or pleased.

“How’s your father getting along, Helga?”

“He’ll be up in a few days. I could take him home if it weren’t for Margie. She’s begged me not to leave her till we know about her father.”

“Could I see her a minute?”

Helga’s blue eyes searched him. “You could, Tony. But I don’t think you’d better.”

“Why?”

“She might say something she’d be sorry for later. Something hard and unforgivable. And it’s all so stupid, Tony.”

“You mean *I’m* stupid?”

“Yes. For saying those terrible things about Blaise Amory. How can you still think them after what happened yesterday? And Margie’s stupid too. For forcing herself to hate the man she really loves."

Tony stared, his face flaming. "That doesn't make sense, Helga."

She gave him a pitying smile. "To me it does. More than once I've heard Margie crying in the night."

"Sure. She thinks something happened to her father."

"She was grieving long before that, Tony Darrow. Ever since she told you never to see her again." Helga looked cautiously over her shoulder, lowered her voice. "You could still get her, Tony, if you'll just go tell Blaise Amory you're sorry; if you're just as square with him as he's been with you. If you'll only . . ."

"I'm not sorry," Tony broke in sharply, "because it's true. And I didn't say half what I could have said. Listen. Amory dreamed up those Ute Indians who're supposed to have scalped nine sheepmen six years ago. He and his gang did it themselves. That foot race to Fort Garland was a grandstand play—just like this big General Amory act of bossin' a search for McCarron."

He stopped, breathless, regretting his outburst too late. Helga looked at him and shook her head. "I'd like you so much better, Tony, if you wouldn't let jealous spite override your common sense. You'd better go, now, before Margie hears you."

Tony found Chuck at the barn and they rode to Alamosa. A letter waited for him at the post office. It was from Receiver Guy Halderman of Del Norte. "A Summitville miner gave me a tip about Saul Spengler," it said. "When you have time come up and we'll talk it over."

The thirty-mile ride to Del Norte took all the next day. The land office was closed when Tony arrived but he found Halderman at his house. "What's up, chief?"

"Blaise Amory," the receiver told him, "was seen in Summitville about ten days ago. He bought a gallon of cheap whisky and rode into the woods with it."

Tony's eyes slitted. "He wouldn't want it for himself. But he'd need it to feed Spengler, maybe."

"I had the clerk at Conejos," Halderman said, "make me a list of all property recorded in Amory's name. One item is a cabin at an old silver claim. It's on the divide a few miles south of Summitville."

"I'll start up there," Tony promised, "bright and early."

"One other thing, Tony." An uneasy look crossed the little man's face. "I'm afraid I've got some bad news for you. About Memphis Jack."

"You located him?"

"Yes, but too late. Sorry, Tony. The man had a

job laying track over Cumbres Pass. Six months ago he got in the way of a dynamite blast and was killed."

Tony had a sinking feeling inside. Here went the last dim hope of ever proving that he, as a boy, had known nothing about the illegal operations of the Tolliver brothers back in Missouri. "How did you find out, Mr. Halderman?"

"His name was on the payroll as John Ladislaw. Nothing to identify him as Memphis Jack. But when I talked with the construction superintendent he said all workers have to fill out a form which asks the question, 'Who is to be notified in an emergency?' The laborer John Ladislaw's form named a sister at Bolivar, Tennessee. He was hired at Alamosa at about the time Memphis Jack paid a five-dollar debt from there by mail. So I wired the sister at Bolivar, which is near Memphis, and she answered yes, her brother was often called Memphis Jack; his body was shipped to her for burial about six months ago."

Tony bit his lip and forced a smile. "Well, I guess that's that. Thanks, Mr. Halderman."

Sunrise found him riding upcountry, heading for the continental divide. A steep wall of conifers lay in front of him and at the very top of it, near timber line, he'd find Summitville. But he was dubious about finding Saul Spengler there.

Because he knew by the map in the Wagon Wheel bunkhouse that the Summitville area had been assigned to Ed Murdy in the dragnet search for McCarron. And Murdy should have stumbled on Spengler if the notary was hiding in a mine cabin.

However, it had to be checked. The sun was an hour high when Tony saw a plowed field off to his left. A crop which had been planted there was weed-choked. Beyond it lay a house and barn—the Phineas Tarber farm.

The house had been locked and deserted since that Sunday in June when thieves had made off with a span of mules.

It was only a little out of his way and so Tony reined in that direction. He could see if anything had been disturbed.

In a pasture Tony found a work team, two saddle horses and a milch cow. They were in good flesh. At the barn and corrals nothing seemed amiss. A pulley well looked inviting and Tony dismounted for a drink. It had two oaken buckets, one of which came up while the other went down.

The bucket at the top was half full. He supposed it had been drawn by the Tarbers before leaving here in June, and so the water in it should be stale. Tony began pouring it out when a splash of it on his hand whispered a warning.

The water was icy cold—not like water which

has stood exposed in the sun. Tony tasted it. Yes, it was not only cold but fresh and therefore was newly drawn from the well.

He looked at the house. Its chimney had no smoke and its shades were drawn. Helga had locked up securely before leaving here in June. Yet someone, within the hour, had drawn water from the well.

Tony went to the house, tried both of its doors and found them locked. He circled, looking at every window. All were latched at the top—but he found one where a small quarterpane had been taken neatly out.

He reached in, unlatched the window, opened it, put up the blind. Here was the kitchen he well remembered, with its shelf of old schoolbooks. But now the room was dirty, with soiled dishes piled in the sink. Helga wouldn't leave it like that. Tony drew his gun and climbed over the sill.

The kitchen air was stale and a whisky odor tainted it. Spengler! A guard had brought Spengler here, Tony thought, counting on a prolonged absence of the Tarbers. On a shelf he saw a gallon jar with about an inch of liquor left in it. A sound spun him around, gun cocked, ready for Saul Spengler's gaoler.

"Come outa there!" he challenged.

A maudlin sob answered him. Kicking open a bedroom door, Tony found Spengler alone and unguarded. The man crouched in a disheveled heap, sweat beading his fat, hairy face. Then, at sight of Tony Darrow, some of the panic faded from his eyes and he breathed what might be a sigh of relief.

"You thought I was Blaise Amory!" Tony guessed. "Amory come to gun you, now that he can't use you any more!"

Spengler's puffy eyes blinked at Tony and his sleeve mopped sweat from his chin. "No such thing," he whined feebly. "I got lost in the woods so I stopped here overnight. On my way to town." The man scrambled to his feet. "I'd better be going now."

He tried to sidle by Tony but Tony's hand pushed him back. "You and I are going to have a talk, fella. A nice long talk about Blaise Amory."

Spengler made an effort at bluster. "You can't push me around. I know my rights. No jailbird range tramp can . . ."

Tony's open-handed slap knocked him to a sitting posture on the bed. "Take it easy a minute while I look around."

He made a quick tour of the house, hoping to find something which would connect Spengler with Amory. But he found nothing, not even the notary seal. A new sewing machine caught his eye, veering his thoughts gently to Helga Tarber. He'd seen it in her spring wagon at Alamosa.

Tony went back into the bedroom with the gallon jar containing an inch of whisky. He set it on a small table. He drew up a chair and straddled it in reverse, his arms resting on its high straight back. "Dropped the seal down a mine shaft, did you, soon as you figured out Amory didn't need you any more?"

Saul Spengler licked swollen lips. His eyes fixed thirstily on the liquor. "I'm a sick man," he pleaded. "Give me a drink."

"Talk comes first. Talk about Amory."

"I don't know anything about him. Gimme a . . ."

"Amory's looking for you right now. Pretends he's looking for McCarron but he's really looking for you. You'd be buzzard bait if I hadn't found you first. And you know it. That's why you sneaked out on your guard and made off with a gallon of booze. Got this far and saw an empty house. So you holed up for a few quick ones and then had to sleep it off. You're lucky at that, Spengler. Lucky to have me for a hangover instead of Amory."

A pale leer creased the notary's face. "If you know so much, why ask *me?*"

"You notarized nineteen titles—all filed and proved up under fake names—to another ghost using the name George Chester. You can't wiggle out of it, because the deeds are on record at Conejos."

"George Chester," Spengler offered slyly, "was an occasional client of mine."

"Poppycock! Your only client was Blaise Amory. What he has on you I don't know. But whenever he brought you a paper you sealed it."

Spengler wasn't listening. His bloodshot stare was on the liquor. "Just a little one," he begged. "That much." He held up an inch of his little finger.

"You can have it all," Tony promised, "after you talk about Amory."

He kept it up all day, Spengler in turn pleading, blustering, whining. By night a tremor of his hands and a thickening of his tongue, plus an increasing hysteria in his voice, warned Tony that delirium tremens might not be far away. An inch of red liquid in a gallon jar was his only hold on the man. "I'd tell you if I knew anything!" Spengler screamed. "But I don't. I'm a sick man, damn you; I need a drink!"

By midnight Tony himself was too weary to keep it up any longer. He found ropes and tied Spengler helplessly to a bed post. "If you change your mind, sing out." Tony went into another room and slept.

Shrieks and sobs awakened him. Shrieks of capitulation from Spengler. Tony got up, washed his face leisurely, went into the other room and released the man. He put paper and pen on the table. All the while Spengler kept shrieking for a drink.

Tony gave him a glass of well water. "The price of anything else," he stipulated, "is a full confession."

"All right," the notary agreed wildly. The thick tongue licked around the lips of his swollen, hairy face. His hand reached for the jar. "Give it to me and I'll tell."

"You pay in advance," Tony said.

The man collapsed on the bed, sobbing. "I had nothing to do with it," he whimpered presently. "Driving off horses, I mean. All I did was seal papers."

"Sure," Tony agreed. "You're too fat for saddle work. Amory didn't do any horse raiding either—personally. But he cooked up the idea, didn't he?"

Spengler went through another cycle through sullen bluster and back to tears. Then: "How would I know who cooked up the idea? He never talked to me about things like that. Neither did Augie Squiers."

Tony picked up the cue. "Squiers was the pick-up man, huh? Amory's gang delivered the stock to a hideout where Squiers picked it up?"

"I guess so. Now I've told you—give me a drink."

"One of the times they did that was a year ago the Fourth of July?"

"Sure it was. What difference does a date make? You promised . . ."

"Wait till I write that down." Tony took the

pen and wrote steadily. He read aloud what he'd written and then put it before Spengler. "Sign it."

Spengler signed with a shaky hand.

When Tony poured a jigger of liquor the man gulped it and begged for more.

"Pay as you go," Tony said. "You've just signed a statement that Blaise Amory planned a horse raid on a certain date. Tommy McCarron was shot dead chasing those raiders. Which makes Amory a murderer in any court. Let's go on from there and talk about Pancho Morales. And Pablo Arragon."

Mention of Arragon brought a new pitch of panic to Spengler. "I know nothing about what happened then! It was before my time." Hoarsely, frantically, the man pleaded his innocence of the Conejos River massacre six years ago. "Morales knew nothing about it, either. When the Indian told Morales, Pancho was scared and wanted to run out. He asked Blaise for a ticket to California. Pancho never did anything worse than file a homestead as Eusebio Sanchez. And I never did anything but stamp deeds."

"Let's get it all down." Tony wrote steadily and patiently, adding paragraph after paragraph to the confession of Saul Spengler.

21

Again it was Saturday in Alamosa. Wagons were in from all corners of the park and every tie rack was full. A shower had settled the street dust and the air had a mountain freshness.

Board walks along Fifth swarmed with shoppers, idlers, spur-jingling rangemen and ladies under parasols. A man came out of a butcher shop with a dressed antelope over his shoulder. A dozen canvas-shrouded wagons were in sight, fresh arrived over Mosca Pass. The influx of immigrants grew day by day—land-hungry men and home-hungry women. Hordes were arriving by train as the narrow-gauge railroad advertised weekly excursions.

Into this focus of pioneer activity, riding east up Fifth, came Tony Darrow. He was leading another horse and astride the led horse sat Saul Spengler. A bleary, bloated and maudlin Spengler whose bloodshot eyes whipped fearfully from side to side as he passed the saloons and shops.

Fearfully as though he knew a bullet might reach out to him, from some unseen source, as one had reached out to Pancho Morales.

The people stared and a chatter of talk stopped. All the county had heard about this derelict lawyer—knew he'd been searched for far and wide. Here he came now in the custody of Tony Darrow.

Tony himself was clean-shaven, almost spruce because he'd stopped with his prisoner overnight at Spalding's stage station. He rode with a six-gun at his thigh and a saddle gun in his scabbard, his eyes alert for Blaise Amory.

A whisper ran along the walks and became a buzz, spreading swiftly from shop to shop, from street to street. Slavick's customers, at Front and State, knew about it before Tony had even crossed San Juan. Simultaneously the story buzzed into the Perry House lobby. Seconds later it was a prairie fire sweeping up Front, licking into Brophy's Bar.

Tony Darrow was bringing in Saul Spengler—marching him straight toward the office of Undersheriff Milt Yeager.

Two men at Brophy's didn't wait to hear more. Wycross and Pinky Mock slipped out to saddled horses and rode for the open range, there taking swift upriver flight toward Wagon Wheel Gap.

At the hub of the town, Fifth and State, Tony turned right and stopped at Yeager's office. He got off, pulled Spengler from the saddle. A hundred pair of eyes saw him march the man inside.

One who saw it had eyes piercing and black and a hawk feather in his hat. He stood with folded arms in front of Slavick's, like a stolidly patient Nemesis. And having seen, Unahwa the Ute turned and strode rapidly out of town, not looking back, like a man whose work is done.

In the marshal's office, Milt Yeager gaped at a signed confession. His gaze veered to a human wreck who huddled blubbering in a corner.

"Is this right?" he demanded, waving the paper.

There was no spine or resistance left in Spengler. His whimpering assent was all Yeager needed. The man who was marshal of the town and undersheriff of the county twirled the cylinder of his gun, checking the loads there. "It's the deadwood," he muttered. "The John Brown deadwood on Blaise Amory."

"Is he in town?" Tony asked.

Yeager nodded. "Just saw his stallion at Wilkins' barn. Nothing I can do but go pick him up. Just as quick as I can write out a warrant." He took a blank and filled out a warrant for Amory's arrest.

"Swear me in as a deputy," Tony begged, "and let me serve it."

Yeager looked at him narrowly. "Ain't you had enough gunfights, fella?"

"He won't fight," Tony argued. "He always ducks the gunplays. Like when he ran twenty-five miles to Fort Garland while his gang was pulling a massacre. Like those Fourth of July horse raids which he left to his men while he sashayed around town with the girls."

“Reckon you got a point there,” Yeager admitted. “Maybe I’d better go pick up Wycross and Mock, and leave Amory to you.”

“I’ve got it coming to me, haven’t I?” Tony pleaded. His earnestness, and the sheer logic of his plea, impressed Yeager. It was Tony who’d been right all along about Amory; Tony who’d lost the good will of the McCarrons largely through the connivings of Blaise Amory.

“It was you turned up the deadwood on him,” Yeager agreed. “I reckon nobody’s got a better right to pick him up than you have. Hold up your right hand.”

Tony held up a hand and was sworn in as an emergency deputy sheriff of Conejos County.

“Now see here,” Yeager directed. “Don’t gun him if you can help it. Bring him in alive. Meantime I’ll go round up Wycross and Mock.”

“You better slap Spengler in a cell first,” Tony advised. He took the warrant and went out.

He hurried down State to Front. There he turned into Slavick’s and asked if anyone had seen Blaise Amory.

Bar talk hushed and customers stared hard at the gun on his hip. A folded warrant showed at his breast pocket and men guessed at once what it was. Slavick answered him hoarsely: “Saw him an hour back. He was headin’ east down the walk.”

Heading, in all likelihood, toward his room at

the Victoria. Tony strode that way himself, past the Alva Adams hardware store, pausing only for a glance into the Peso de Oro. Half a block further he went into the Victoria Hotel. "Amory in his room?" he asked the clerk.

Here too whispers had been rife—about Tony bringing in the truant Spengler. Now here was Tony inquiring grimly for Amory.

"Might be," the clerk said. "Key's not in his box."

Tony went up the steps and to the door of room seven. His knock wasn't answered. "Amory!" he shouted. "The law says open up."

Still no answer. Tony kicked the door open, found the room empty. But riding gauntlets were on the bed—further indication that the man was in town.

As Tony passed out through the lobby loungers, a brittle silence followed him. Every ear had caught the command about the law saying open up. Talk crackled again, leaped to the street, crossed to the bank and to the depot, spread east to China Pete's brothel and west to Brophy's Bar. Tony Darrow was the law, it said. His witness was Saul Spengler. A warrant was in his pocket and he was looking for Blaise Amory.

Minutes after the Victoria knew it the town knew it. Knew it as surely as though the Singing Dunes themselves had whistled it from the hills.

Tony Darrow circled the block, inquiring

here, there, everywhere. He stopped at the Perry House, at Conkley Brothers Corrals, at Struby's, at Stevens' Drugstore, and even at Brophy's Bar.

A man at Brophy's snickered. "No, we ain't seen him, mister. But Wycross and Pinky just skinned outa here, hellbent for the tall sage."

Tony swung back up to Fifth and turned east again. He was passing Easterday's grocery when he thought of Spengler's office upstairs. A bare chance that Amory was hiding up there. The Jaybird man by now would have heard the buzzings around town. A stern contempt for him filled Tony. It would be like him to skulk rather than stand and fight.

Tony took the dusty steps two at a time and again kicked a door open. No one was there so he hurried to the street again. As he turned toward State a hand plucked his elbow.

An excited boy whispered: "I just seen him at Shaefer's, mister. Watch out for him. He was buying a gun."

Tony went on to Shaefer's in the next block. "Amory left here about five minutes ago," a clerk said. "Yes, he bought a Colt's forty-five. And some shells for it, Mr. Darrow."

The irony of it brought a sardonic smile to Tony. *Mr.* Darrow, they were calling him now.

He went on to Hunt and down Hunt to Front and then patrolled west again. Again he looked into the Peso de Oro. Then on to Slavick's. A teamster watering at the trough there offered a warning. "Look out, brother. He's right around the corner."

It was only three steps to the corner and Tony took them cautiously. Two railroaders coming out of Slavick's bumped into him, knew him, dodged discreetly back into the saloon. Tony looked north up State and saw deserted sidewalks, eloquent testimony that people expected them to be swept, any moment, by bullets. This was the block where Blaise Amory, on the first Saturday in May, had put on a one-man parade with sidewalk crowds applauding the fancy stepping of his horse. Over there was the Perry House, from whose upper balcony Margie had watched the exhibition. The fleeting thought of Margie put Tony for a moment off guard. He came back to realities when a bullet fanned his ear and a gun boomed up the walk.

A second shot came and Tony spun around that way, his own gun out and cocked. Blaise Amory had stepped from O'Brien's Oyster House. A madness of hate made his face livid as he held a two-handed grip on a gun, tripping its trigger, pumping bullet after bullet. Tony walked toward him, matching shot for shot. "A warrant for you, Amory. Better drop that gun."

Only the first of the man's bullets came close to Tony. He shot his gun empty just as Tony's last bullet smashed into his chest. Amory staggered a step, tried to get back into O'Brien's. He got the door open and fell inward on the restaurant floor.

Frightened waiters grouped about him. One of them looked up and saw Tony standing there. Tony blew through the bore of his gun, reloaded it, put it back in the holster. The hollow voice of a waiter came to him. "You got him, mister. He's dead."

22

When he'd made a full report and answered every question, Tony rode wearily back to his homestead on the Conejos. "Heck of a pal you are!" Chuck greeted him sourly. "Not lettin' me in on it."

"I'm going to sleep for a week, Chuck. Anybody shows up to see me, throw 'em out." Tony bathed in the river and went to bed.

Chuck Gleason stood guard over him and turned many away, including a reporter from the *Rocky Mountain News* who'd come all the way from Denver. But two callers were too important to be denied, in Chuck's judgment, and he let them in.

The first was a committee of three representing the citizens of Alamosa. Its chairman was John Moomaw who ran the jewelry store and led the town orchestra. His fellow-committeemen consisted of two popular musicians known as Simon Frank and Banjo Joe.

"We held a meeting," Moomaw announced, "and decided what you need is to cut up a few didos."

"A belly laugh or two wouldn't hurt, Tony," Banjo Joe added. "You been too busy dodgin' slugs to have any fun."

"We remembered what you said at the inquest," Simon Frank put in, "about how you learned to play a fiddle. Coupla horse thieves gave you a few lessons, when you was a kid. So the least we can do is make sure you got a fiddle." He brought forth a long, mysterious package he'd been holding back of him, presented it to Tony.

Tony's eyes were moist as he took it, caressed it gently. Here was a fine violin and he'd never had one of his own. "You shouldn't 've done it," he protested feebly. But he put it to his chin and struck a chord. "Listen, Chuck! It's a dandy!"

"And here's something else," Moomaw announced. He handed Tony a promissory note for a thousand dollars—one that Tony had signed to the bank at Alamosa. "Paid in full," was written across it in the hand of Cashier Camp.

"The San Luis Park Live Stock Association," Moomaw explained, "have a standin' reward fund for catchin' stock thieves. You sure caught up with Blaise Amory. So they paid off your note at the bank."

The other important caller came a day later. He was Guy Halderman and Tony greeted him with a grin. "Am I still on your payroll? Or maybe you don't need me any more what with George Chester all washed up."

The little gray man from Del Norte smiled. "The job's yours as long as you want it, Tony. There'll always be an illegal filing here and there. Fact is I've a dozen suspicious cases right now over in the San Juan Basin."

The San Juan Basin lay west of the continental divide. An idea sparked Tony. "Look, chief. I'd like to get away for a while. Clear out of the park, I mean. Too many people want to pester me with questions over here. So why not let me ride those San Juan filings for the next few weeks? Over around Parrot City, are they?"

"All the way to the Utah border," the receiver said. "Sure, Tony. You can write your own ticket. I'll send you a list of filings over that way. Start any time you want."

Two mornings later Tony rode west, leading a pack mare. He topped Cumbres Pass and followed the railroad to the end of track, which by now had reached nearly to Chama. Sight of the track-laying gang brought a wry thought to Tony. If he had looked among them a year ago he would have found Memphis Jack.

His third night out he camped on the Rio Blanca. Two filings along the Blanca were on his list. Tony checked them and in each case found a family living in tents, busily building shelter for the winter.

It was the same, a day further west, with claims on the Piedra. Riding on, Tony spent a week checking land filings along the Animas, below Animas City. Intense excitement prevailed there, where the oncoming rail line was scheduled to end, and where boomers were already staking out a terminus city to be called Durango.

Tony found not an off-color filing till he got to the Mancos, where four brothers had filed adjoining homesteads although only one of them as yet had come further west than Omaha. Doubling back to Parrot City, Tony mailed a report on this to Receiver Halderman.

The Parrot City postmaster handed him a letter from Chuck Gleason.

> . . . Couple of U. S. Marshals grabbed Wycross and Mock in Wagon Wheel Gap. Mock went green under the gills when they mentioned Mark McCarron. They kept working on him till he offered to turn state's evidence to save his neck. The marshals didn't promise a thing but they wrangled it out of him, just the same. Mock claims McCarron was shot by Trigger Huggins in the Jaybird barn, with Blaise Amory standing by. Claims the body was tossed into La Jara Creek a mile below the ranch, and the sheriff's down there dragging for it right now.
>
> Margie's all cut up, naturally. But every single male in the park is out to cheer her up. Especially that sharp-looking young foreman of hers, Luke Priddy. Luke was

> Tommy's best friend, as I remember, and he always was right close to the McCarrons. So you better come home and mend your fences, fella, before it's too late. Anyway Margie sure needs plenty of comforting, these days, being all alone there. The Tarbers went home to their place near Del Norte.

Tony lingered long over Chuck's note. Then he wrote one himself, painfully and awkwardly—a note of sympathy to Margie McCarron.

From Parrot City he rode back easterly, making land checks on Florida Creek and Pine River. His journey was six weeks old, and the higher aspens were turning yellow, when he rode into Pagosa Springs.

The postmaster there gave him a letter from Guy Halderman.

Tony opened it—and what he saw made his heart jump.

> . . . the look on your face hurt me, Tony, when I told you Memphis Jack was dead. So I tried once more.
>
> I had a government man in Tennessee call on the sister. She said her brother spent a week with her just before he left the last time. A few days after he'd gone a letter came for him. She had no idea where

he was so she put it in an old grip he'd left with her—and forgot all about it. The government man asked to see the letter and they opened it. It was from Podge Tolliver and here's a quote: "We hear you're going west, Jack, and we want you to do us a favor. Stop by and pick up Tony and take him with you. We got to thinking about what you said. You're right. It's not fair to the kid to keep him here with us, him not knowing what's going on."

This wipes your slate clean, Tony. I've sent a copy to the governor of Missouri and to the judge who presided at your trial. You'll hear from them both—and from anyone here in the park who ever doubted you. . . .

Tony's heart thumped and a tear ran down his face. When he rode on, a pain was gone and it would never come back again. For the first time in years everything was easy and sweet inside of him.

A mile beyond Pagosa he came to a trail fork. The right fork would take him to Cumbres Pass and Conejos; the left would be a more direct route to Wolf Creek Pass and Del Norte.

The right fork would take him quickest to Margie; the left to Helga Tarber.

• • •

Again a wide-tired wagon went creaking down the mountain, under brakes, the strong gloved hand of a girl holding the reins. The team was horses, this time, instead of mules. Again the wagon bed had been removed and thirty-odd smooth spruce poles loaded lengthwise on the running gear, forcing the driver to perch atop the load itself. This fall afternoon was warmish and she wore no jacket. Her honey-yellow hair had lost some of its pins, due to a day's work in the wind. With her free hand she tried to rearrange it, then gave up and instead loosened it completely so that it showered forward in golden cascades over her shoulders. She made a bright picture there. Her denim pants, tucked into boot tops, were navy-blue and her shirt was a gay crimson.

The trail was narrow, a gap barely wagon-wide down this steep forest aisle. Turning a kink of it Helga Tarber saw an arch of bleached ribs. "Steady, Danny!" she cautioned as the off-horse shied.

It was the skeleton of a wolf and it made her think of Tony Darrow. Here he'd come riding out of the forest and into her life. Would she ever see him again?

His voice startled her. She turned and there he was, asaddle by her forewheel. The way he looked at her brought a wave of color to her cheek. "I was hoping to see you, Helga." His hat was off, his dark hair sweat-matted. A rope from his saddle reached back to the halter of a pack mare.

"Tony! Where did you come from, Tony?"

A smile broke the tired lines of his face and his words came joyously. "I'm sure in luck! Right where I found you before. You sure look fine. How's your pa?"

"He's coming along wonderfully. And you?"

"Camped last night on Wolf Creek Pass," Tony said. His horse dropped a jaded head. "He's trail weary," Tony added with a bold gleam in his eye. "Maybe I oughta take a weight off his saddle."

When she smiled and moved over a little, he tied his horse to the wagon. The pack mare would follow of her own accord. Tony climbed the load of poles and seated himself beside Helga. He took the reins from her and slackened the brakes.

The wagon rolled on down the aisle of pines. For a mile neither of them said anything. Helga stole a glance at his lean profile and saw a look of contentment there. He was more relaxed than she'd ever seen him before.

His head turned and their eyes met. Loose yellow hair framing her face made Tony say: "I saw a picture of you once, in a book somewhere. Only you weren't on a wagon. You were on a ship. A Viking maid, I think they called you."

Presently they came out of the pines and could

see all of the park spread before them. Tony Darrow looked out over it with shining eyes.

"Helga?"

"Yes, Tony."

"Did you ever play make-believe?"

"Lots of times, when I was little."

"Let's play it now. Close your eyes."

She closed them and he closed his own. "Now let's pretend we're in a covered wagon wheeling over Mosca Pass. We can see millions of acres down there—free land waiting for us—and we can take our pick."

"It's beautiful!" Helga murmured. "I can smell the pines above us; and the sage below us. It's a wonderful land, Tony."

"We're wheeling down the pass," Tony said, eyes faithfully shut, "and we can hear singing down there. Great dunes of sand humming and whispering. They sing, 'Come into the park, Tony and Helga, and find yourself a home.' "

She felt his arm slip around her. A wheel hit a rock and the jolt threw her against him. His arm tightened and she knew it wasn't make-believe at all. It was real. This *was* their wagon of fate and ahead lay their land, waiting to welcome them home.

Center Point Large Print
600 Brooks Road / PO Box 1
Thorndike, ME 04986-0001 USA

(207) 568-3717

US & Canada:
1 800 929-9108
www.centerpointlargeprint.com